W9-AGC-715

LOVE LOVE and LOVE

Sandra Bernhard

HarperPerennial
A Division of HarperCollinsPublishers

A hardcover edition of this book was published in 1993 by HarperCollins Publishers.

LOVE LOVE AND LOVE. Copyright © 1993 by Sandra Bernhard. All rights reserved. Printed in the United States of America. No part of this book may be used or reproduced in any manner whatsoever without written permission except in the case of brief quotations embodied in critical articles and reviews. For information address HarperCollins Publishers, Inc., 10 East 53rd Street, New York, NY 10022.

HarperCollins books may be purchased for educational, business, or sales promotional use. For information please write: Special Markets Department, HarperCollins Publishers, Inc., 10 East 53rd Street, New York, NY 10022.

First HarperPerennial edition published 1994.

Designed by Jessica Shatan

The Library of Congress has catalogued the hardcover edition as follows:

Bernhard, Sandra.
  Love love and love / Sandra Bernhard. — 1st ed.
    p. cm.
  ISBN 0-06-016615-0 (cloth)
  I. Title.
PS3552.E73142L68 1993
818'.5409—dc20   92-56229

ISBN 0-06-092551-5 (pbk.)

94 95 96 97 98 ❖/RRD 10 9 8 7 6 5 4 3 2 1

This book is dedicated to my grandmother
Edith Lazebnik,
an extraordinary woman
who passed on her love of storytelling
to my cousin Faye Moskowitz,
who in turn passed it on to me.

There is nothing
like the blessings of your family
to help you remain truthful to yourself.

A very special thanks to: my family, as always;
Cynthia Mort, for her support and guidance;
Daniel Chick, who I will always carry in my heart;
and Patricia, for her inspiration.

"What's the things you like most in life?"

"I like lots of things
but there are three things I like most,
love love and love."

—ANITA EKBERG in *La Dolce Vita*

LOVE LOVE and LOVE

INT. LIVING ROOM.

ALISON sits in a chair and speaks directly into the camera.

ALISON: I had the weirdest dream last night. Actually it's a recurring dream. I board a plane, and all the seats have been replaced by banquettes, some set in corners, curved. The seating is haphazard so I sit wherever I can. We start taxiing down the runway which in reality is a two-lane road. The plane is lumbering along forever, like it's trying to get up the power to get off the ground.

BACKGROUND MUSIC UP—Dusty Springfield singing "The Look of Love"

We take off, but immediately we are headed into high-tension wires. We are now in a tunnel and we're going to have to pull back just as we leave it to avoid the wires. Well somehow we just miss them but of course some other obstacle will present itself again.

FADE OUT.

FADE IN.

A woman with long dark hair is sitting up in bed. A cigarette is lit by a match.

The camera pulls back to reveal a sleeping figure next to her. The woman, JACKIE, blows smoke down at the pillow causing the figure to stir and wake.

JACKIE: *(shaking the person)* Wake up!! I have to talk to you. I can't sleep. Come on, talk to me Alison. You start this big conversation and then you go to sleep. I don't want to sit here alone. You know I hate being alone.

ALISON: *(freaked out)* What the fuck is wrong with you? You scared the hell out of me, will you please put out that fucking cigarette? Jesus I was just dreaming about you.

JACKIE puts out the cigarette, picks up a martini glass and drains it.

JACKIE: Was it a good dream?

ALISON: No. You were really cold and angry with me, and smoking in my face. Why are you awake?

JACKIE: I hate you so I can't sleep.

ALISON: Oh, that's nice. What did I do now?

JACKIE: You went to sleep and wouldn't fuck me.

ALISON: Okay, fuck you!!

JACKIE: You're a bitch and I hate you.

ALISON: This is lovely.

ALISON gets up suddenly, throws back the comforter. She storms out of the bedroom, making sure to turn off the alarm, and goes into the living room.

INT. LIVING ROOM
ALISON curls up on the couch.

ALISON: *(yelling)* Jackie why are you so cruel? What is the point of staying with me if you can't stand me?

JACKIE, naked with huge tits, comes into the living room. She appears dirty.

JACKIE: I'm leaving darling . . .

She teeters away, as if she's wearing heels, and goes into the den.

INT. DEN.
ALISON, wrapped in a wool blanket, follows her in.

ALISON: Do you want me to help you pack all your pretty things?

JACKIE pushes ALISON hard against the door.

> JACKIE: If you don't want me to kill you darling, I sug-
> gest staying out of my way. *(begins to scream, like
> a harpy)* I don't need another fucked up mother
> telling me what to do. . . . You're so stupid it
> makes me sick. Look at you, a weak fucked-up
> dyke.
>
> ALISON: You're the one who loves to eat my pussy
> when I have my period. Don't you think maybe
> *you're* the dyke?

JACKIE, with ALISON following, walks out of the room.

INT. BEDROOM.
JACKIE frantically packs horrible aqua toreador pants and
midriff blouses purchased in street bazaars in Paris into a
trashed suitcase. She puts on a T-shirt, Gigli slacks, and
pumps, and begins carrying her suitcase out to her car, a
old Toyota Corolla in dead green.

> JACKIE: *(smoking and schlepping)* Don't touch my
> bags. I'm going to check into a motel and then find
> a place in the morning and then I never want to
> see you again.
>
> ALISON: *(exhausted)* What is this, the fifth time in a
> month you've tried to leave in the middle of the

night? Why don't you just go to bed and we'll talk about it in the morning.

JACKIE: *(crying)* I don't know why I let you talk me into coming here. I knew you wouldn't take care of me the way you promised. I'm incredibly fragile, you know that. I'm still recovering from my addiction and can't be pushed. It's not that easy to decide what I want to do. And I'm too scared to write again, I can't handle the rejection.

JACKIE takes ALISON by the hand and leads her to the bed.

ALISON: *(not sincere)* But you're so talented, you should just go for it.

JACKIE: I hate that expression. It reminds me of all your mindless friends from the Valley. Oh . . . hold me.

FADE OUT.

FADE IN on the LIVING ROOM.

ALISON: *(speaking directly into the camera)* I was desperate when I met Jackie—I was on a mission. You know, I had this certain image in my mind of the kind of woman I wanted. I wanted someone in a Chanel suit, shoulder-length dark hair, super successful, a little eccentric, well-traveled, nice breasts, sensual mouth, a little cold. A friend of mine knew this girl, Jackie, so late one night we

5

did a three-way call to her in Paris where she was working as an editor for this . . . alternative fashion magazine. She had this great accent that at the time really impressed me. She told me she had ridden in the rodeo, described herself as very waspy. . . .

Beat, ALISON remembering

. . . She smoked like crazy and drank too much, did heroin. She told me that's something you do in private, part of the drama, I guess. Sometimes at night I would wake up and she would be way on the other side of the bed, completely in a world of her own. I would lean on my elbow and watch her. It hurt me the way she slept away from me, so I would make some noise or try to move near her, but that always felt so incredibly desperate to me. So after a few moments I'd get up and walk out to the living room, watch the trees move until I felt drowsy enough to go back to sleep. . . .

Beat.

. . . She always asked me to hold her. She never held me. I was remembering that the other day, and I never asked either.

Love is the only shocking act left on the face of the earth. Eroticism, murder, betrayal, starvation, torture, war, all pale in the face of love. We stare for hours at CNN, watch the world unfold hour by hour, numbed, deafened, defeated. We wander into the wrong neighborhood and are showered by hatred. We study the universe through distant cameras, drive ourselves mad searching for the origins of life. We detach ourselves and engage in futile superficial conversations about sexual politics, impressing one another with intellectual repartee, dress ourselves in various guises to avoid the alienation of aging skin, exchange hostile glances in loud, desperate nightclubs. This is the dance, the prelude to need and desire.

We confess our sins in cold, damp churches, kneel to the Lord to open our souls, punish one another for the frailties we cannot bear in ourselves. Winding ourselves up into frenzies of fear and self-loathing we are tamed by a cocktail or hallucinogen, pretty colors, strange desert journeys, emptiness and abandonment.

We flee from this most terrifying moment: in a warm

room in the quietest night with whispers of tenderness and trust penetrating the senses, control, power, anger are thrown aside and we bear witness to the only valid instant in the universe, love.

I'm being held captive by a group of thugs. A middle-aged man has my arm pinned behind my back and is cutting the top of my wrist with a hunting knife. I'm screaming in agony and fear as I feel the blood oozing down my arm. "Why are you doing this to me?" I cry. Next thing he wants is to fuck me. I tell him I will if he wears a condom. I can't find any but keep looking as he wraps some kind of soft plastic fake brick around his penis. I'm looking in a bottom drawer in my parents' room and there are surgical gloves, scalpels, and condoms lying on a towel. I take out a rubber and put it on his erection, and his cohorts all scream at him, "What the fuck do you think you're doing fucking her?" Then my father is making my bed in his bedroom in Flint, I tell him I'm scared of getting AIDS. He says, "You'll live three hundred sixty-five years, you'll live to be five-thousand years old." I'm suddenly in Saddam Hussein's entourage being swept away to a Swiss bank. I realize I'm right next to him, so if he gets shot I will too. Trying to pull back is impossible. I am cheek to cheek with him as we enter the bank. A honeycomb bullet-proof shield is quickly put in front of us. All bank employees have their hands up in the air to prove they are weaponless. We run like a herd of cattle down a hallway into the vault. The look on everyone's face is that of awe and deep respect. I cannot believe I am a part of it.

Casey was dreaming, kind of jerking in her sleep. I was watching her, knowing that she had to leave in an hour and that I might not ever see her again, not like this anyway. Her purse was sitting next to the bed—it was tempting to look inside. Ever since we met on an MGM Grand night flight to L.A. and I realized she was traveling with an older man who Was Not her father I was desperate to know who she really was. She would soon be on her way again, but where she came from and where she was going I most likely would never find out. Even so, looking at her now I was sure I knew her in a way few others were ever allowed to.

She was exhausted after getting her navel pierced, which was, by the way, unbearably sexy. We laughed like young, crazy girls while she stood in my bathtub pouring a bottle of hydrogen peroxide over her stomach to prevent infection. As she slept I ran my finger over her rubbery red red lips which, she confided to me the first time we kissed, had been injected with silicone.

Casey was a small girl with bleached blonde hair, who one simply could not ignore. And I didn't. I spotted her in the lounge at Kennedy clutching the same purse I was eyeing now. She took out a Marlboro and lit up, and we smiled across the room. I was laughing at the dummy sitting at the Grand piano, she caught me, and it was the perfect segue for me to walk over.

She told me she was a model (albeit a short one) and I assumed she was on her way West for pilot season.

"No, no, just going to hang out! Isn't that cool?"

Well, I can't say I thought it was so cool, but she was sparky and beautifully tough so of course I went along with it. Her sidekick, an older Jewish man in the "paint business," or, as I later discovered, the "pain business," came over and broke up our burgeoning flirtation, and I was none too pleased about it. But I figured he might have saved me, so I was polite and went ahead and boarded the plane.

I was sitting in a cabine with a woman who lucked out and got on this flight along with a stack of five Ray's pizzas bound for L.A., and a guy in promotions with a record label I soon forgot.

Apparently Casey and her pal were in the process of getting upgraded and one of the seats happened to be with us in the cabine. She jumped right on in and the guy left her there for the remainder of the flight, never once coming back to say hello or discover us in positions, that, had I been him, would have had me asking for my money back.

She had all of us going for most of the flight, using the

airphone to make sure her "boyfriend" in Minneapolis paid American Express so her kitty's vet bill would be covered. Casey was feeling rotten because she had left a window open and the cat caught a cold, and apparently it was sneezing and everything. So here she was on her way from New York, but really living in Minneapolis with this guy who traded precious metals, belonged to AA, was possibly a member of the Witness Protection Program, and extremely jealous. All in all, not a great profile.

We all talked through dinner, and by the time the movie was ready to start Casey and I were playing footsies with each other. She ended up next to me, whispering in my ear, telling me about her lavender Baretta pace car with flames that she bought outside St. Paul, talking the guy down to $13,000 from $18,000.

"You should get the companion car in aqua," she said. "I can help you get a great deal."

I was seriously considering it when she slipped her tongue in my ear. The woman with the pizzas looked kind of sick but the record guy was amused.

By the time we touched down I sensed I was already in a bit too deep and felt sad when the old guy took her away to the first of many hotels with Beverly in the name. She told me to call her at the Beverly Hills Hotel, which I did the next day. She met up with me at a dinner I was having with a bunch of girlfriends who agreed she was cute but thought that perhaps I was a little crazy. We made out in the alley behind Carl's Market and I drove her back to the Beverly Wilshire where she was obligated to give the old fart a blow job.

I drove home seriously questioning my sanity but picked her up for lunch the next day at the Beverly Hilton. I asked her about the hotel change and she started crying, telling me she had gone horseback riding and left her purse in her escort's trunk and he wouldn't give it back. She seemed hung over but wired, and I was getting nervous and incredibly tired thinking about the drive over Coldwater Canyon.

We spoke the next day and she broke down again, because he made her move to the Beverwill Hotel, which was not exactly a lateral move, because she had pierced her navel. He screamed at her, "You're nothing but a little tramp, a spoiled fucked up brat. I can't stand to look at you right now." So he put her in exile.

She confessed to me that he was supposed to be paying her $1,000 a day, but was reneging on his part of the bargain. I suggested a day job, but she asked me where could she make a thousand dollars a day, "At Denny's?" I couldn't argue.

She came over that afternoon and we made love and I could tell she needed this love very badly. She fell asleep in my arms—as if she hadn't slept in years—and I hated to wake her. But she had a plane to catch, her job was over, and she was going back to New York to stay with an older woman who did this for a living—getting free dental work for blow jobs.

She got into a Valley cab for the airport, and as I hugged her goodbye I remembered her birthday was coming up a few weeks later. Both of us were crying because everything had been so fast and insane, and because I thought I might be able to save her from it all. But when she closed the car door and the taxi pulled out of the driveway I knew she was already trying to put me out of her heart. By the time she took off I was probably out of her thoughts as well.

I tried to find her here and there. In New York at some crazy number, at her boyfriend's in Minneapolis—a guy who sounded like he might be brandishing a knife at someone's throat at all times. And when I sent her a bouquet of flowers on her birthday and the only address I had was Highway 7, I could feel those cold winds blowing through my open window.

I finally got a hold of her. She politely thanked me for the flowers but cut it short, since her boyfriend was standing there.

Two years went by before I heard from her again. I thought of her from time to time, hoping no one had murdered her or done something just as final.

When she called she seemed like a different girl, she had lost her edge, that excitement in her voice. She told me she had married her violent boyfriend but they had already divorced. She was now in recovery, finished with her cocaine habit, and she had colored her hair brown.

"I just wanted to let you know I'm doing well. I've been through a lot and did so many crazy things."

I felt like I had been one of those things.

She seemed judgmental, as the reformed often do, and it made me not like her anymore. Missing the fucked-up beautiful girl who passed through my life briefly but with such resonance. It was like she had left a part of her true nature in little piles along Highway 7; if I were younger I might sweep them all together and reassemble her lost heart.

I think I want my next lover to be Indian, dressed in rich oranges brocaded with gold threads, slender fingers that will intertwine my own, thick puffy lips like divine pillows brushing across my cheek, sitting cross-legged in the kitchen waiting for the curry to simmer to perfection, chewing on an anise seed gently brushing back her thick black mane of hair. She draws me in with hands on my face, kissing me deep and long forever on my mouth, breathing into my neck, murmuring such sweet inaudible words of desire. She makes love to me on the cold kitchen floor, cradling me in her soft silky arms so tender, so strong, unrelenting, delicious. She smells of jasmine and orange water, incense and rare spices.

Last night I had a dream about a party that was taking place at Diane Keaton's. She was really warm but shy. It was a kind of art gathering, showing these paintings, maybe for some magazine. The crowd was fabulous but not obnoxious. On a lower level, not exactly a basement but down some stairs, Mara was sitting with a Japanese man, her hair had been sheared incredibly short and it revealed a long thick scar on the back of her head. I said I'd never noticed that scar before, but she didn't respond to the remark, as she was focused on the Japanese man who took off his shirt. His body was flaccid but she didn't seem to care. I felt very left out and nervous as if I had lost her to this guy. I got up to go back to the party and rubbed her head, well I'm going to run, I said, nice meeting you to the guy who was cold as ice. Mara's eyes were kind of distant and glazed over. I took a deep breath and went back to the party. Diane, who was being subtly flirtatious, asked me if I would ever consider making love to her. I felt very centered and told her, yes, anytime. At this point everything became very chaotic, the party was ending but people were milling around. I wanted them all to leave so I could be alone with Diane. I had kind of undressed and was searching for my bra. I noticed a box with two puppies playing so I took them out, but they weren't that cute. I was just going to start kissing Diane in her bathroom, where clothes were drying on racks, but we got interrupted or I kind of woke up. But then the dream continued with me trying to squeeze through a small space, to get back into her house. The garbage trucks were coming around collecting and there were a lot of fumes in the air. I felt very calm and at some point noticed Mara again with her hair longer but still not that long. Her back was to me so I couldn't tell what her attitude was. Then she turned around and all of a sudden it was Diane, but by then I had lost interest in both of them.

IF I had known she was hunched over the toilet bowl, of course I never would have asked her. But I didn't know.

"What would you do if you were here right now?" I twisted my hair and sipped some cold water. "Would you touch me, kiss me really hard, penetrate me, stroke my neck? Don't you love my neck? Isn't it you who always sings the praises of my skin?"

There was a long pause and she cleared her throat quite hard which struck me as strange, so I dropped that course of conversation.

"Are you all right honey?"

Her skin was quite remarkable. She had never once gone in the sun and it showed. It was creamy white with soft hues of peach in her cheeks. I thought of that now, before she could catch her breath to answer.

"No, I'm not fine at all—so angry."

She said it so softly I almost asked her to repeat it, but I heard it clearly in her quietness.

"Why are you angry?" I asked, afraid that it was something so ancient that no one, not I nor anyone qualified, could help.

"I've been throwing up on and off all day. I just finished when the phone rang."

With that she laughed a little bit and I rolled over on my stomach, the phone cradled between the pillow and my head. For the first time ever I felt helpless and at a loss for words, seized by the sensation that I couldn't help her—and that I didn't want to either.

"Well, what do you do when this happens?" My mouth felt dry, the words echoing without care.

"I can choose to stop or maybe my heart will tear loose and come out of my mouth and for one instant I'll be able to watch it beating in the toilet before I flush it and my life away. Maybe this time I'll stop it and go about my business until the next time when I care less or more depending on how you look at these things and only then time will tell. What would I do if I was there right now? Hold you too tightly, drive you away, close in on you, scare the shit out of you, but that is what I worship about you—your strength. I love to see my weakness consumed by it until I almost disappear. Can I come over tonight, please?"

It would have been impossible to say no, so with some hesitation and a bit more regret I told her to come over at nine.

When she walked in she made sure I noticed her bandaged hand.

"I burned it on New Year's Eve lighting an exotic drink."

I felt sleepy, wishing someone would come take her away. She insisted on showing me the burn which really wasn't so bad. I examined it from different angles but couldn't respond. The silence hung there like rotten air. And just as I was ready to suggest she leave, she got up, all teary-eyed, and with bad posture walked out the door.

I exhaled deeply, realizing I'd been holding my breath since she got there. A cool glass of Arrowhead water felt like a stream running though me, and the tiny flickering light bulbs in the living room reminded me that help was on its way and that perhaps next time I might keep my heroic urges to myself.

Drug addicts
Call Girls
Tragic Heroines
I will find them
On flights from New York
In Paris cafes/strip malls in the Valley
I can't bear to be alone.

I was walking last night, alone but not particularly lonely. The wind was cold and slapping my face harder than anything I'd ever felt, but I continued to move. A German shepherd ran out into the street, then saw headlights moving toward it. I screamed out to the dog, smacking my red, chapped hands. I scared the dog so badly it ran back onto the curb, the car swerved and the driver shook his fist in a fog of breath out the window. The dog was shaken and slinked over to me. I crouched down on the curb and she rolled over on her back crying, so I began to rub her stomach causing her leg to flutter. She was a sweet little pup, very young with that downy fur on her belly. Her lips fell back as I scratched her, revealing clean white sharp teeth. I have to say I felt like a child, recalling all the great dogs we had growing up. I put my face close to her snout and she kissed me so sweetly.

"Hey, what are you doing to my dog, seducing her or something?" His voice scared me, knocked me on my ass. "Oh Jesus, I didn't mean to freak you out."

A very attractive young boy was smiling down on me and it made sense that this was his dog.

"Well I guess this all looks pretty bad doesn't it, a girl making out with a German shepherd on the street, but I swear it's not what it looks like. She was almost hit by a car and I, well, kind of saved her life. Naturally she was attracted to me and I figured I owed her a kiss at the very least."

He laughed, sat down next to me on the sidewalk, and lit a cigarette.

"I understand, but I'm extremely jealous of anyone getting close to Cheri. That's her name, Cheri. I confide everything to her and she's young and impressionable. You might be misleading her, you know."

"You look younger than Cheri. Maybe I could mislead you as well."

I took a puff of his cigarette and tasted something sweet.

"That's entirely possible."

He stood, put his hands underneath my arms to pull me up. Cheri was climbing on top of me, gently biting him.

I brushed off my pants, he wrapped his scarf around Cheri's neck, and I said, "Do you want to come over for a drink or something?"

"What's the alternative, going back to my twin bed alone and thinking about you?"

"No, I don't think that would be at all acceptable. Hmmmmm . . . did Cheri tell me your name?"

"She would have in a minute. Josh. I'm Josh, and I'm

not joshin' you . . . and I don't care what your name is, just don't leave me tonight. Please."

I didn't tell him my name and I didn't let him go that night either. His body was, well, smooth, long, strong, extremely warm. I couldn't close my eyes all night, watching his head on the pillow, Cheri next to him. They were snoring and lovely to look at, both of them.

"Why aren't you sleeping? He asked in a sleepy voice. "I'm the one who should be awake, touching you. But it feels so safe here I just kind of drifted away. Something keeps pushing the blanket away and I can't push it back down, so maybe I won't be sleeping anymore either. Do you think you can help me with this uh . . . little problem I'm having?"

He rolled over to me, pulled me close. Cheri jumped to the floor.

"It doesn't look like such a little problem to me, I think it might take some time to solve." And it took all night.

It doesn't hurt to be alone sometimes, I found myself thinking as I threw on a sweatshirt and walked Josh and Cheri to the door. To go out on a cold night and walk for awhile. It might be dangerous, someone could hurt you, there are sad scenes, passersby who leave a lifetime along the way for you to pick up and examine, papers blowing in the wind with strange messages, maybe something hopeful that you save and cherish forever.

Jackie Stone had no morals or regrets on the morning before Lawrence tried to kill her. She stood behind him as he shaved in the mirror, a can of menthol Edge seemed a poetic addition to the retable. Jackie caressed his bare chest where water, shaving cream, and bits of whisker dribbled down from his chin, she rubbed his nipples and cooed.

Now this irritated Lawrence because he was a very busy and important man living in a world that accepted no excuses for being late or tired, and he was both of those things this particular morning mainly because Jackie began arousing him somewhere between 3:15 and 4:45 A.M. so intensely that three individual sex acts were performed in rapid succession: her, him, and both. The last encounter involved Jackie straddling Lawrence with a mixture of resentment and anger. It hurt him, but that was good for a man who lived a life that demanded a total denial of emotion.

It was Jackie's sexual audacity that brought them together in the first place. She had shown up at 1:45 in the morning, drunk out of her mind, the first week they met.

He was so furious he sent her home, but the realization that few woman would have attempted that with him stuck in his mind and *elsewhere*. And when they compared notes of their sexual prowess, more like two men than members of opposite sexes, and she remarked for dramatic punctuation that "she could fuck him in half," he was hooked. That remark haunted him, and led, of course, to this point, to the morning before he tried to kill her.

She caressed his chest now violently and he told her to "Knock it off"—he was late, nervous, and it wasn't cute.

She had huge hair, kind of dry and in need of a good trim, and smoky breath that bugged him always but especially early in the morning. In spite of that he allowed her to smoke in bed and sip martinis late at night as she connived and brooded and he futilely attempted to sleep.

"But darling I don't want you to go to work today. It's too predictable!"

She jerked him backward, causing the razor to slip and gash his cheek. Not only did she not apologize, she kicked him in the back of his knee and knocked all of his products into the sink and onto the floor, shattering glass and spilling expensive cologne. He, on the other hand, grabbed a fluffy white towel and pressed it against his wound which was bleeding profusely down his chest and onto the floor.

"Oh God, what have you done!" he cried out with a voice not unlike the broadcaster who witnessed the explo-

sion of the Hindenburg, as if to exclaim "oh the human-
ity," which was instinctively the very right thing to feel.

Jackie pushed him to the floor where he landed on the
bath mat. He was crying now and even later for work. She
undid his towel to begin rubbing his thing, which amid the
blood, fear, and confusion became incredibly hard. She
put it in her mouth and did what was her claim to fame,
did what kept Lawrence right there with her—she gave
him the blow job of his life. She also managed to get in a
few choice words about what a loser he was, "so weak and
spineless" and that when she left him, which was just a
matter of time, he would "shrivel up and die like an abandoned dog."

With this barrage of insults and amid the carnage, he
let loose in her mouth—she gagged, and spit it in his face.
She lay next to him rubbing herself until she came too.
When he finally managed to stand up, he crawled into the
shower, letting hot water run over his body.

She went downstairs to the kitchen and made some coffee. Lighting up a cigarette she tied her robe tightly
around herself, smiled and exhaled. Lawrence came down
dressed nattily as always in a suit with vest, blow-dried
hair, and a big gauze bandage across his cheek.

She kissed him and fixed a piece of toast. "Oh darling I
love you so!"

He was appropriately silent, breaking it only when he
honked the horn of his Mercedes and suggested that per-

haps they should discuss the morning's occurrences tonight on his return.

"Really, Lawrence, it wasn't any big deal. Why are you flipping out about it?"

He looked scared, possessed, confused as he drove away into town.

He called once during the day but hung up when he heard her voice. His jaw clenched and he slammed the drawers to his massive desk. His young, modern assistant, a pretty blonde who knew when to keep quiet, knew instantly what was happening.

At home Jackie searched through her Chanel bag for birth control pills and a little bag of heroin which she smoked later after a luncheon of salad nicoise delivered from a restaurant. She called into work sick after he left, and told his maid to clean the upstairs first. She then called a girlfriend and described the morning's activities. Throwing her hair back and forth, she talked about some hustler she was hot for and how she was going back to Paris as soon as possible. She thumbed through a Marguerite Duras paperback throughout the conversation, laughing occasionally but without much enthusiasm.

The day went on like this for both of them. He ran to lunch and avoided any explanations, talked on the phone, made deals. His cooler partner walked in and swung the door closed, bracing for another horror story. Lawrence cried again, Tommy tried to reason but soon grew weary of this now familiar scenario.

When he returned home that evening at seven he found Jackie, curtains drawn, in a deep sleep. He stood by the bed watching her breathe, he carefully carried away a full ashtray which he flushed down the toilet.

She was sitting up in bed with a light on when he walked back in, sheet up to her chin, the outline of her breasts pressing against it.

Reaching over, she brought his hand to her lips and kissed it. "Oh darling, I've missed you today."

Lawrence felt shaky and began kissing her on the mouth.

"I'm not good for you Lawrence, I'm thinking about going back to Paris soon. At least there I can find my way around, sit in cafés, smoke and read without anyone torturing me about it. I can be dirty there, go without showers—I'm so sick of taking showers! Your life is closing in on me—it's a fucking drag darlink! Will you make me a just perfect martini? oh please? And I'll love you forever, besides you never take me anywhere and I hate you for that. Everything here in its place. Lawrence, one day you'll come home and I'm going to have things all moved around so you can't find them. I'll make stains on the couches, break the Limoges, fuck you up darling, maybe then you'll relax!"

Lawrence's breathing became labored, pulling at his

hair he stormed out and noisily prepared her a martini. Carefully putting two olives on a toothpick, he brought it in on a silver tray.

"Oh, you are an angel. Did you fix one for yourself?"

Lawrence took a sip, then suddenly drained the glass. He threw an olive at her, and started laughing.

"You asshole! That was my martini!"

She threw back the covers revealing cheap nylon panties cut low, and the sagging breasts of a girl who developed too quickly, too young. She grabbed a shirt, wrapped it around her, and knocked the glass out of his hand, shattering it against the wall. He lunged for the stem.

Staring her right in the eye, "Come one inch closer, Jackie, and I'll cut your fucking throat!"

"You fag pussy asshole! Come on try it! You're just a little lady, you wouldn't have the guts."

He knocked her back on her ass and fell on top of her. He wrapped his hands around her neck to strangle her, but she managed to unzip his pants anyway, extracting his penis. Moaning and shaking, struggling with her panties, his eyes bulged; barely holding his grip, his face moved in closer to hers, then her tongue met his lips and squeezed its way into his mouth. Gagging, he relented and pressed against her body with all his might. She was incredibly wet so she brought him inside without hesitation.

The house was quiet. He could feel the pounding of her

heart so he covered his ears. She was crying now but he sensed the tears were false and that made him hate himself more than her. Carefully he picked her up. Carrying her downstairs he opened the door, and set her on the porch. The Chanel bag followed and he quietly locked the door. He thought of calling the police but knew it would only get uglier.

As he vacuumed up the shards of glass from the carpet the sound of her fists slamming against the door unhinged his brain. So he let her back in and fixed her a bath. And a fresh martini.

They slept soundly quite close together, hoping he would figure out what to do in the morning.

In spite of her darkness, which she cultivated with great originality and commitment, a certain light shone through that she would have gladly extinguished had she been aware.

She was not at all what I expected when we met after a brief courtship on the phone. How does one put a face and voice together? Hers was melodious and seductive. Late at night I would take her number off a worn yellow page and dial with great reverence another country, another world. I suppose I invaded her life. With my usual overconfidence and persistence I convinced this total stranger that she must meet me in New York in a week and a half. What the hell was she supposed to think? But that never entered my mind on this mission to seduce, to be loved.

We met on one of those very dark, rainy, cold New York March nights. Little time was spent talking before I pulled her toward me, an impatient gesture of lust and desire. And although one would have thought it a disaster, the night was truly amazing. I fell in love with her on the spot, amid the pristine Philipe Starck setting, sheets of rain lashing the penthouse windows. A misrepresentation of my conservative nature perhaps, but I have not regretted it for a moment.

She smelled everything and kept some things just so she could recall the bad odors and times of childhood— you know, those smells that take you right back to a certain time and place: your mother blotting a spill, your little brother vomiting down the side of a wastebasket; you running crying from your parent's room when you found out your father had angina; sipping sherry the nights you babysat around the corner, talking on the phone to Micky, a married man in Phoenix, laughing and kicking off your heels as the kid called out for water and Micky was squeezing his balls to keep from coming. You listened, really loving him. You turned the Dusty Springfield record to the "The Look of Love" as he told you how hard his cock was. You shot some Glade mist into the air and watched it fall inhaling deeply the pine forest scent. You could have been with him up in Flagstaff; he offered to fly you up in his private plane, but "some other time" you said, your father was going in for open-heart surgery and you didn't want to rock the boat.

Micky wore Brut and Old Spice deodorant. You met him at tennis lessons. You couldn't believe he was almost forty any more than you could believe you were only eighteen.

You drank Sprite from nubby bottles as he caressed the back of your neck, working out some knots. Sitting in his Alfa he put your hand on his hard-on and you just loved it. Of course there had been others, but his bent backward with a determination you'd never experienced. The car was so hot you burned your elbow on the dashboard. Kissing you for a while you begged him to finger you. It got so out of hand, really. Your hair, straight brown to the shoulder, damp, smelling like Breck shampoo and conditioner, glossy lips that tasted like bubble gum, you always kept them so shiny, they left a ring around his penis like something a good detergent couldn't remove.

That's how it started two days before your father almost died on the table but pulled through with more energy than ever before, so much so that he left your mother for some fuck bunny at I Magnins. You had seen her there, floating between the shoes and purses, when your mother bought a bas mitzvah present for Jodi, a gorgeous bag that ran $130 at the time, outrageous but very cool.

Yes, daddy left and you got bitter with Mom which never really made any sense. But in spite of it all you kept seeing him anyway, never making the comparison between you and daddy's new chick. Besides, Micky's wife was a JAP bitch who never wanted to fuck him, not like Mommy at all.

I was typing in my office the other day and one of those hideous two-prong bugs fell out of my sleeve; the sneaky little bastard tried to get away and I kept flicking at him to knock him off my desk. I finally succeeded and knocked him right into a spider's web. It was unbelievable. As quick as I've ever seen a spider move, this little fucker descended onto the two-pronger who was flippin' and floppin' to try to escape, and oh, this little spider was just as grand as could be, attitude to spare, whistling away some sick, scary little tune: Yep, I got you two-pronger and I'm going to busy myself all over your ugly ass tying you up nice and neat.

I sat there watching this whole thing go down, listening to the spider and the obvious silent terror of the once know-it-all two-prong bugger. I watched for a minute or two, and I have to admit I was disgusted by the spider's relentless and cruel behavior.

So I finally stood up and walked over to them and said, "No, spider, you will not kill that mental two-prong bug. As much as I hate him, I will not give you the satisfaction. I'm going to kill both of you pathetic creeps." And I

kicked them onto the ground and crushed them both with
my foot, grinding them into the industrial carpet. I finished my typing and walked outside, sleepy in the sun,
uninspired and hungry.

I call my mother from the bathtub. I figure that way I can keep it short, because I'll have something to blame it on—you know, "my hands are shrinking up like prunes," laughter, love you, then get out, dry off, go on with my life.

But of course it's never like that. I hear her voice. "What's going on Mom? You sound a little down."

"Oh, nothing, I just saw some kids playing around here today and I thought poor me, I miss the kids."

"Well, I bet they live around there Mom, and don't forget you can always get on a plane and visit us, any of us. That's the great part."

I can see her sitting on the couch in the den, the modern Italian very-difficult-to-fold-out-the-bed couch. I wonder how long she's been sitting there, napping in front of the TV, going to the fridge with a Kleenex stuck up her sleeve, making a snack, the louvers closed, the house dark (she doesn't want to fade out the carpet with the Arizona sun), all her art work jammed in everywhere. It drives me nuts, but then it's not my house or my life and as often as I go home to see her, it's really none of my business. But it kills me just the same, the clutter to keep the loneliness at bay.

Somewhere across town my father lives with his wife and never calls my Mom, which I know is for the best; but it leaves the whole family in limbo, in a place where there was once a sense of security, however false, a place we still secretly long for. The missing limb of emotion, you swear you can still feel it, the soft strokes, the sharp pains.

Mom gives me the rundown of her week: to the movies with Lola, you should see how limber she is, she sang in the chorus with Fanny Brice, posed for *True Stories;* Elaine and Ed are hosting a seminar on how to sell your art; there's a family New Year's gathering at Ruth's; lunch with cousin Diane; Ken is off on a business trip.

I'm soaking and listening. She wants a comforter for her bed which is king-size but "just get a queen because it's only for me." I send her a big hug and a kiss and so much love every part of me has shrunk in the bath.

Everything in my house is perfect. Slowly that drives me mad too.

She has little memory of it now. Oh, sometimes when she's falling asleep the sound of metal ripping into the ground, the smell of acrid smoke, the odd silence may ring in her ears, but generally her dreams do not haunt her. And although she often holds the picture of her parents above her as she smokes a cigarette in between papers and books to be read, she has a strange detachment to her past.

Marnie is a strangely beautiful girl, which is a kind of predictable way of describing someone who seems to have a style of her own and a confidence that rings true in all situations.

She has just started parting her hair in the middle, and has pinned a lot of pictures of Penelope Tree and Twiggy above her bed. She burns incense and listens to the Doors and everyone at Smith respects her strong opinions and clear insights into these times.

At a recent rally against apartheid she climbed onto the roof of the Literature building and read old speeches from H. Rap Brown over a portable speaker while Nina Simone played under her. In a particularly expressive moment she chose to rip the string of pearls from around her neck and throw them at the group.

———

"This is not a case of pearls before swine," she screamed out, "but a pig has more respect for life than we do. We are the privileged, the sought after, the great minds of our generation, and yet we watch the world go down around us and let our mommies and daddies clean up our shit and our guilt. I for one will not stand for it. The sixties may be over, you can call me a romantic idiot, but I will not sit back without taking responsibility for my own actions and some of yours as well. We've got to tear this world apart, we've got to recall a more causative day and spark the fire of revolution once again. I am so fucking mad."

And in her fury she jumped two stories and tore her jeans in all the right places. All the girls screamed and told her she looked really cool.

"That is not what I tried to achieve, you assholes." She licked the blood off the back of her hand and walked away, shaking her head of all the thoughts that overwhelmed her.

The girls didn't really get it, some of them in smart slacks, some in Laura Ashley dresses, most dreaming of great jobs in New York or of marrying sexy young men with great jobs in New York. The world was too overwhelming.

"What can I do?" a small girl in a down vest and topsiders said to her friend.

"Well, you know Marnie's all fucked up. How normal could she be?"

"I don't get it. She has everything at her fingertips: the best family, the greatest boyfriend, she gets invited to every right event in the world, and she wants to be like Angela Davis or something. It's weird, like she's from another time zone, but God she's brilliant."

"**Are** you in mourning again, crying over old lovers?"

I swung around and lightly slapped her face.

"Come on, what's with you? Jesus, you're such a beauty. I can sit and stare at you for hours and think, what if I were Aaron? How many amazing places I could go to with that face? But then I fall asleep and somehow I know that it must not be easy. So I respect you even more and love you dearly, I do. I only wish you would stop crying because you've inspired me to get better and better. Come on, let's get out of here—some fresh air will do you good. Then we'll come back and play some records, dance like we did in high school and maybe not even talk, just dance and have a drink. You know we always communicate best when no words are involved. I never feel lost with you. Let's walk for a while—you always feel better after you walk. I love your feet. Have you ever noticed how you walk one foot directly in front of the other? It gives you this kind of majestic stride. It's royal, absolutely royal! Would you breathe a little bit? Christ! It's as if you would shatter if the wind blew on you. A little walk and some breathing, that's my suggestion for you.

———

Stop all this intense shit. Larry is a loser and you know it, but for some reason you have always overlooked your best qualities. For example, your feet, the way you walk. Don't allow these little morons to control you, Aaron. I'm going to be forced to punch your arm incredibly hard if you don't snap out of it. Look, either I give you a bruise or I drug you and take you downtown for a tattoo. That's it! Why don't I treat you to a nice little bleeding heart with five tiny drops of blood oozing out of it? Let's put it on your lower back or thigh. Kooky lambooky—oh wait—did I just see a smile race over your lips? I can't believe it. You are stunning, a real pain in the ass, but a total knock out. Let's drink a couple of scotches, take a taxi downtown and get you a nice tattoo, and I'll get one too. A thorny rose on my ankle that will serve as a constant reminder of what a tortured soul my best friend Aaron has become."

A woman who read my last book told me that when she finished it she thought to herself, "This is a very unhappy person, I really hope she finds love in her life." She told me this at my brother's house in front of my sister-in-law. She caught me completely off guard and I felt extremely uncomfortable. I thought about it a lot while writing this book, what she'll think of me now.

I recently purchased a large bottle of acidophilus & B. Bifidum capsules at Mrs. Gooch's on Coldwater Canyon. I put them in the refrigerator. A few days
later I was packing my vitamins all together for a trip to
New York and London, and I noticed the bottle was not
only unsealed on the outside but the inner seal was
already stuck under the top when I opened it. Normally I
would have thrown out the entire contents immediately,
but trying not to be an alarmist I mixed all the vitamins
together along with some remaining acidophilus capsules.
I took a shower, but it began gnawing at me, the possibili-
ties of the capsules having been poisoned. I dried off,
applied lotion, put on my plaid flannel bathrobe, and went
back to the kitchen where I proceeded to sift through the
vitamins, separating all the acidophilus and returning
them to the original bottle. On the way to the airport I'm
going to take them back to Mrs. Gooch's and ask to
exchange them for another bottle.

Nostalgia for suburbia, the way love was supposed to be, incinerators, picking up scratchy AM radio stations late at night from thousands of miles away, sleeping in the back seat, dreaming with the comforting sounds of passing trucks on an interstate, the lonely faces of the drivers moving silently along the highway staring, lost in a hypnotic state, thinking of boy's penises, soft, lonely too // losing touch with old friends, recalling their faces, smiles, the way they smelled, lying on a twin bed on the other side of the room listening to them breathe in the night // the sound the wind made in the back yard without opening the drapes to see, drinking cool water from a Dixie cup, drying off in the sun on the grass next to an inflatable pool, the ID bracelet from Jim wrapped in a piece of brown paper the way he gave it to you sitting in the bottom drawer, the son of a rich lawyer you talked to quietly when your father went to buy you a bulldog puppy, the strawberry blond jock who sat behind you and never took you seriously even when you told him you liked him // the dust horses kicked up on 68th Street, stars, constellations, the moon you could never figure out but watched, walking with friends at night, the quiet house when the boys had all left for school, the taste of greasy food stuck to the roof of your mouth, the fifth important lover listening to these stories with tenderness, and you believe for once someone is finally loving all that you are.

Gabriella told us not to look into the garage. "It's too dirty in there, honey." Something in her voice told me I was better off remembering what it used to look like when Dad's Sedan De Ville was parked there.

I stared at my reflection in the window, recalling the night the garage door froze shut and we huddled together, my three brothers and Mom, waiting for Dad to come home from Boston. Time stood still until it opened again.

Never had I seen any neighborhood fall apart like ours. It bore no resemblance to the cozy street where I played, hiding in well-groomed back yards, tossing acorns behind me. Now the kids seemed mistrustful, frightened, shyly avoiding eye contact while riding bikes on buckled cement sidewalks.

The house had just been sold so it stood empty. The redwood stained fence that had separated our yard from Ben Kaufman's was gone. A giant satellite dish sat there in the shrunken back yard, so did the totem poles Mom made and placed there in 1964. The patio was tiny now, still imbedded with the tiles she had set into the cement. The ceramic light covers were intact, a bird's nest resting on top of one along side some rotting wood exposed from the storage room.

The deterioration shocked me, Gabriella, my brothers Mark and Dan, and their wives, Claudia and Carolyn, all of whom had heard the stories of 3110 Concord Street as if they were legends handed down by the ancients.

This is where we grew up and where we spent the fourth of July 1992, trying to piece together the lost years after we moved away in '65. I wondered if it would even be standing if we came back again in another ten years. I felt as if I left my reflection forever in those garage windows as we pulled away.

I met him at the Pink Elephant in 1977, long before it became a club of chic late-eighties detachment, when it was still just a funky, gay, beach bar. In from Virginia looking for a friendly face, he was a photographer who gave me a strikingly hollow self-portrait that I've kept under a pile of stale underpants in a bottom drawer along with a stolen menu from the Nickodell restaurant on Melrose that I thought I might use as a piece of art in my Norton Avenue apartment. His eyes were crazy, and he sported a droopy mustache, kind of like John Lennon in the late sixties. We danced to Gladys Knight, he whirled me around the small, packed dance floor to the Eagles and Joan Baez, who was going through her Streisand period. (One night I raced out of a sound sleep down the Santa Monica freeway at the urging of my Mexican hairdresser and partner-in-crime, Willie, who had placed an urgent call to inform me that Joan was indeed there, dancing with a really butch-looking woman. When I got there she was sweaty, wearing a tank top, drinking something harmless, and talking quietly to this unknown woman. I stood transfixed, the melody to "Diamonds and Rust" rushing through my head.)

He whirled me around and we drank tequila and kissed until I felt sick, which didn't take long. He had nowhere to stay so we went out for breakfast with Willie at the Lion's Den coffee shop on Lincoln at one a.m. Willie left, I brought him home with me. I drove—with a haircut just growing out badly—my green Maverick with the landau top my father gave me when I moved from Arizona.

I made him keep his underpants on. I could barely sleep thinking maybe he would stab me in the middle of the night. I woke up to him going down on me. I smacked his face and he rolled over, angry and sullen. I laid there as the light slowly filled my room with all the loneliness one feels waking up to a not-so-perfect stranger.

He woke up confident, smiling and asking what was for breakfast. He put on his pants that smelled smoky and I brushed my teeth and drove us to Canters. I felt sick and detached from anything I thought I would be feeling when I imagined love and romance in my adolescence. I sat across from him feeling vaguely like a girl, not at all like a woman, feeling more or less like some gangly teenage boy who had no concept of his power or charisma. I kept thinking, what could this guy possibly want from me? And although he called me for a while and asked to see me again, I avoided his invitations.

I saw him again waiting for the bus at Santa Monica and Fairfax near the Alpha Beta. I was stopped at the red light, he was borrowing a match from some girl in a halter top and talking quite a bit from what I could tell. I felt hurt in some weird way, as much by myself for not letting him like me as by him not being able to convince me to. Maybe I needed to make myself more feminine.

Jerry Pillars was right down the street and I parked in front. The racks were jam packed, tight with designer dresses and gabardine slacks. I had to knock some things on the floor just to see what was there, to find that one special piece. A woman in high-heel sandals, flared gabs, a French cut T-shirt, and an LV bag thrown over her shoulder ignored me and fingered a chemise top that I kept eyeing. I noticed her nails, the square tips and juliette wraps painted in a color I guessed to be Misty Plum—it reminded me that I was about to be late for work at the salon Cia where I had manicures booked back-to-back all day long. The thought of my 12:30 pedicure with that woman from Palm Springs who never cut her toenails in between her once-every-six-weeks appointments was enough to make me cry.

I looked up at the boxes of Charles Jourdan shoes marked down from $125 to $49 and suddenly felt the world closing in. I couldn't breathe, everything was starting to look cheap and whorish. I felt panicked, like I couldn't bridge the gap between my self-imposed feminine exile and the deep desire to sip a glass of wine with some internationally alluring man, to be charmed and indulged without a second thought. I settled on a raw silk blazer and skirt ensemble and a pair of mock lizard strap sandals with thin heels—not a great heel in retrospect, but right on for the times (or 1978).

I wrote a check and felt so good driving in to Bev Hills to work. Dulcie, the blonde, wispy-haired woman who got a face peel every year on her vacation and who spoke in nasty nasal tones and booked our appointments, was in particularly good spirits. I took it as an omen when she said, "Sandy, you have a new client today, a real nice-looking fellow too." It was something she might have said to any young girl, and I swore she was looking over my shoulder speaking to someone else. I turned around to see who it was and I caught my reflection in a mirror obscured by a hanging plant. I was convinced that this day would change everything.

She was at the very least magnificent. She was big and black and angry at me, screaming from the dressing room obscenities I had only heard once in my childhood from an adjoining room on a family vacation at Caeser's Palace in Vegas. It was sex talk to someone you might as well have been stabbing to death, and I didn't like it any better today than I did at thirteen on my way to see Diane Caroll singing at the Sands with my parents.

"You ugly white cunt, where are my diamond chandelier earrings? Must you insist on being as stupid as you are ugly?" She screamed at me teetering on her new Blahnik mules, her hair under a stocking cap, as she grabbed me by the arm, pressing in hard with her nail extensions. "Now don't cry, cry baby little white wanna be something Jew girl tryin' to run away from the past and do big special things like dress this SEXY GORGEOUS BIG TITTIED FUCK BUNNY EBONY BLACK AS NIGHT BLACK AS COAL GRAND CHANEL DIVA! Do I see a tear forming? Not on my time bean pole, shapeless fool, toothpick with two BB's. What are you hiding under that burlap sack child? Come on, wipe off that forty years in the desert face, and get up and put on my wig and allow me some time to unwind, sip a Remy and get in the mood to ENTERTAIN. My people are waiting, this is Manhattan, the night is dark and fierce and I must (she dragged me to my feet) I MUST shine tonight because people are laying out those American Express platinums to witness the one and only Miss Ember! (She ran frantically around the dressing room screaming into her reflection then back at me.) I'm burning, I am on fire, I'm ready to explode!"

By mistake I started singing under my breath, "Don't tell me not to fly I simply got to. If someone takes a spill it's me and not you."

"Hush your mouth, child. That voice is destroying the atmosphere. You sound like someone is trying to push you out a twenty-one story building onto the street below and you're begging for your life. Shut up!"

She led me into her dressing room, the holy domain, the inner sanctum, where sometimes if I arrived early enough to the theater I would sneak in to pray at her altar, finger the racks of evening dresses, hand-beaded velvets and shantung silks, some gifts from designers who were fans, others custom made by the people who dressed the theater. I would stare into the vanity like Natalie Wood did in *Gypsy*, proclaiming out loud to the emptiness of the universe, "Mama, I'm pretty, I'm a pretty girl."

One time she caught me but let me go on for quite a while before she terrorized me and set me back to a pre—bas Mitzvah state of mind.

"Homely child, whatever are you doing in the privacy of my boudoir? What in the living hell do you call this invasion! No no no, do not even attempt to open that vulgar mouth of yours. Why can't you go out and get yourself something new to wear? Call that rich son of Abraham, Isaac, and Jacob, physician heal thyself, fucking the nurses, turn your ugly little girl into a no account nigger-dressing dyke daughter father of yours and ask for some of that inheritance now! Head off to a sample sale, or Loehmanns and pick yourself up a frock that doesn't feature your entire lunch all over its tattered second-hand nasty-ass front. Go on now, Orphan Annie can't respond to save her life, ugly, ugly little freak of nature, go on now, gather my wares and help me do what I do best—teach the people all about high grand Diva Style, Grace, Beauty, and SexUality. Have you figured it out yet, you kosher Cinderella? Quickly now, midnight is approaching, I wouldn't want you to lose your special appeal and turn into a bigger pumpkin than you already are. Fasten me, child, hook up my brassiere!"

She was exceptional that night. I never grew tired of hearing the songs, "Fodder on My Wings," "Sugar in My

Bowl," "See Line Woman." She was on a Nina Simone jag that season and became obsessed with putting fresh cut flowers in each room.

As for myself, I was everything she described: self-loathing, young but no kid, dirty, disorganized, at odds with my family, stubborn, introspective, horny, possibly for another woman, a fag hag, living on the Upper East Side in a postwar building, alone in a studio where I played my Striesand collection incessantly. I slept on a futon that destroyed my back, ate Hebrew National hot dogs, and dreamed of being like she was, A Real Lady, and, of course, a Grand Diva as well, for in spite of how she tormented me, I could sing and quite well at that. I narrowly missed out on an open audition for the New York City Opera—Beverly Sills herself told me that I just lacked a little of the power big boobs gave a girl. She put her arm around me and told me to study, that I was darn good. So I went to Jim Gregory, an old-time vocal coach on 47th Street, right around the corner from the Palace Theater, two flights above the Fundador Spanish restaurant and the June LaBerta dance studio. I went twice a week and sang two hours a day, received monthly checks from my father, a Merrick, Long Island, internist who appeased me with money, which of course I resented him for and didn't want to depend on, so when I read about Miss Ember opening for an extended run off Broadway I applied for the job of dresser, assistant, and abusee. For some unknown reason she chose me and it was there my life pivoted and the amazing brutality and brilliant tutelage began.

There was my very scary, mad period which lasted for at least thirty years. Sudden depression, melancholy, loneliness. You know, the usual—bursts of anger accompanied by intense sadness.

It was one night in particular when everything came to a head. Memories of childhood traumas, people who had left me, sirens screaming in the distance. A dog hit by a car, a little puddle of urine forced out, a dribble of blood running out of its mouth. The retarded kid who waved her hands above her head behind the chain-link fence in Flint. Sunday afternoons winding down into night, my mother's fragility, my father's obsessiveness, my brother's fears, the sweetness of Yiddish grandparents, timeless modern furniture, leaping down five stairs in an act of triumph, a thousand endless conversations with fictitious comrades, lovers, and business partners, wasted relationships, abandoned plans and dreams, rewards, successes. You know, the usual.

It started coming faster and faster. The thoughts wound around one another like the inside of a baseball, rubber bands of thought wrapped around a hard rubber core. I let it all go, to unravel without judgment or regret. Numb, at times vomiting, shaking, shitting, contemplating razor blades in a dramatic moment to produce some blood, not much, just a little something to leave a scar on the top of my arm, nothing more than a deep scratch, but that passed and was overlooked for the predictability of it.

Finally I managed to call my mother, who by this point had garnered an amazing amount of strength for someone who was like a leaf hanging onto its tree for dear life. She listened and I could feel her gentle hand on my forehead, like my grandmother's hand scratching my back until it turned bright red. Hands, oh, I remember everyone's hands, and I felt my mother's love then like I never had before, it soothed me and I wanted so much to let go of my demons, my dybbuks. When do you release them, when do they let you rest? I asked her. And she told me that they just do when you don't need them anymore, and I prayed for that moment because there have been times when they went away for a while. My mother's words soothed me, everything receded back into some serene spot. I slept, finally, dreaming about round edges and my mother's hands. I try to stay there whenever I can, until I have a child of my own to soothe and take away the madness and the pain.

Down the block at the end of Blix Street, where it forms a little island—nothing exotic, keep in mind, just big, metal telephone poles shaped like the Eiffel Tower, where there are broken rocks, craggy and jagged, clumps of dirt and hair, some deserted cans, bottles, instructions for microwave ovens, flyers for sales at low-priced boutiques—wanders a Mexican man. Maybe he'll wait for the bus, crouch down on his haunches and shade his face from the sun. Some dust blowing off Vineland, he rubs his eyes.

On the other side of the island the street changes its point of view, moves past Riverside, beyond Moorpark, and up to the base of the hills of Studio City, but right here, turned toward me, a Mexican man is waiting. A little girl in a lavender confirmation dress walks toward him but continues past with her mother to do some shopping at the Ralph's up on the three-way intersection of Camarillo, Lankershim, and Vineland. I never go there because all the cheese looks old and usually there's only cheddar, but many people in the neighborhood do.

The Mexican man is blocks away when I return. Where he had rested there remains a spot like some great archaeological find. Who knows, when the earth shifts again and some species disappear perhaps they'll dig up the ruins of North Hollywood and carefully dust off a bit of aluminum, a rusted hairpin, and people will talk quietly of who was here when the Mexicans roamed to Ralph's.

Matthew was one of the men I ran into along the way in one of those towns I can't remember anymore, like Cincinnati or St. Louis, or maybe Des Moines. I was moving around quite a bit then, like a gypsy in a caravan, a one-man band playing these stinking little clubs for four to six hundred a night. The usual crowd, local fancy girls on a big date, tall handsome strong guys, overconfident, loud drunks. Everyone was getting laid but me and I liked it that way, because I was already feeling detached enough living in these comedy condos and Red Roof Inns, driving my Plymouth Volaré, crisscrossing this great nation that was turning into a muddle of dirty browns and ravaged greens.

I usually drove alone and I carried a gun that I had to use when a club owner set me up in the parking lot with a couple of guys who tried to rip me off my $1,200 in cash. They backed off quickly, but after that I threw the gun into a garbage can at a Sunoco station on some dismal turnpike knowing all too well I was probably on the verge of using the damn thing.

So I hadn't been with anyone in nearly a year when I met Matthew. He was a bartender at the Comedy Cavalcade, but he said he was getting ready to start a program at one of the DeVry Institutes to become an engineer, which appealed to me because I knew only doctors and dentists through my family; it seemed exotic and lonely and that's what first attracted me to him.

He watched me every night I played this place that was filled with lots of fake wood paneling and swirly gold mirrors. I could see his distorted reflection from the stage as I told one liners and went off on crazy knee-slapping tangents, and sometimes I would lose my place when I could see that he was really laughing and enjoying me a lot. It touched me because it was rare that guys who worked in these dives actually listened or even talked to you once they knew there wasn't going to be any sex involved.

When I walked off stage after the late show on a Saturday night he came out from behind the bar and put his arm around me and, well, frankly, it felt just wonderful. I hadn't let anyone that close since I left my dog with a girlfriend back home, and it startled me. I could tell I was going to cry very hard some time in the next twenty-four hours while he confessed all the cruel things he had done to women in his life: the ugly girl in high school who worshipped him and sucked him off in the locker room after a big football game; the girl he almost married but who had suddenly lost her appeal and he dumped without ever saying sorry; the countless ladies who had ordered cocktails in the five different bars he tended since giving up the dream of becoming a high school coach, the ones who threw themselves at him without any pride or dignity and whom he used without any feeling whatsoever. It was like listening to some song from a passing car, I could only make out every few words but the melody was familiar and I kept humming it over and over as he continued.

At one point, I can't remember when, I reached over and kissed him on the mouth. It tasted like peppermint schnapps. Without a word I took his hand and we walked outside crossing the street to my motel.

He kept looking down at the pavement repeating, "I don't deserve this."

"And just what do you think you're getting honey?"

I can't say it was the best sex I'd ever had, but then again sometimes the look in a man's eyes that betrays his deepest fears makes up for the quickness with which everything happens. That look lingered for quite a while, I have to say, and by the morning it seemed to have changed both of us. He rode around with me to three or four cities and we had a lot of fun—and sad—times. Like the first day when he pulled off the road and squeezed me so hard I took on all his regrets. We couldn't separate but realized we wouldn't be together long. I soaked his shirt with my crying because, like I said, I knew I'd be crying some time soon.

You can really go places once you know that some of

those sad moments will eventually fade away. That's about the time I began to know it, and that's why now, as a big success, I can't recall the city where I met Matthew.

In Rome they want you to eat Ritz crackers like some fucking gourmet treat.

I sit waiting in a restaurant that I am the first to enter. The waiter serves me reluctantly like I'm twisting his arm. I want carnae melazone, eggplant stuffed with meat, because I had it here the week before last and I had a taste for it.

But he gets angry and tells me no, and throws an English menu at me that explains all the dishes in the most simplistic terms, and doesn't even list the specials. I throw the menu onto the next table, and if anyone is watching me they might observe me telling him to fuck off.

I order ensalde mista collette Milanese, mezzo, aqua minerale con gas. I crave meat and it tastes good. I ask for angouria for desert, even though the watermelons are always hit and miss—this one kind of misses. I eat it quickly because I have to be back in my hotel room by two. They are calling me to let me know if I will work this afternoon, but I won't. So I go back to my room and sleep, having woken up at six-thirty this morning to get on the set.

I would do anything for a massage or a good fuck.

Waiting, forever waiting to work on this film. Today I wake up to a phone call from a lover. We talk, as usual, about the decrepit state of our relationship. But I am incredibly sexual and so we have phone sex, although we're interrupted at least five times by incoming calls. The hotel operator cuts in on the word "clit." And believe me—I'm not trying to draw this out—I just want to come because I know for sure it is going to be another long day here in Rome. It starts to get really hot again when suddenly I hear a man with a black American accent cut in.

"Hey get off the line, will you?"

"Why? I put my two hundred lira in first."

He finally gets off, I'm sure in more ways than one.

Why is it in London I wasn't horny once but in Rome that's all I am? There just isn't any distraction here I guess, so why not jerk off.

I finally come, hang up the phone, and get out of bed.

Bob, an old friend, calls to invite me to lunch, which is great. He has two sons, and one, Chris, is very cute, but he's leaving to go back to Paris this afternoon. Too bad, I say. Bob seems stunned. Hey that's my son. No shit Bob, and he's cute, and if he wasn't your son, well, you get the picture.

But on the up side, the son and I go to check out this mind-blowing church I've heard about. You go in, pay this Franciscan priest a few thousand lira and the fun begins. The entire place, lanterns, wall decor, chairs, is made up of human bones. Thousands of scapulas make up a collage, more bones create a kind of makeshift lounge area for the skeletal monks in robes, sitting in various and sundry positions, holding crucifixes. Some are standing, ready to walk off their boney pedestals and right into the confessional.

Today it was unbearably hot and I was unbearably alone. I woke up only to quickly eat my calazone and quickly fall back, deeply, into the hardest sleep I've had in I can't remember when.

I dreamt that Mom and Dad, or some semblance of them, were traveling somewhere on a fast, bustling train, discussing their impending divorce with a lawyer. Suddenly there is a quick cut, and I find myself sitting in a lounge waiting for news about them and the crash. A lot of people died and I kept holding a young college girl on my lap who was like a combination of my sister and my daughter. I held her tight—I had to be strong for her but I would burst into tears each time the rescue team brought out another body. David was there, a kind of presence, and there were a few young girls, I seem to remember three. Finally someone explained that it had been an Allegheny flight that had crashed, not the train. I was convinced that Mom and Dad and the lawyer were dead, but finally a car pulled up and Mom got out of the back seat. She seemed incredibly strong, stronger than I'd ever seen her, and really happy. I was so relieved to see her and yet strangely unsure of it. I went to her and examined some bruises she had endured in the crash. One wound in particular, on the back of her neck, was raw and open. She tired of explaining how it happened and I was crying so hard. Then another car pulled up and in it was one of the bulldogs, maybe the last one we had. I held him in my arms, but he was just a head, a giant olive that had been eaten around the part that was his head. He was alive and I was so happy, but again I cried hysterically. Then the phone rang—it was Isaac—so I never found out if Dad survived, which has been bothering me all day.

It was hot as hell this morning and I was reeling from the heat when I finally got a cab. I took the cab to the synagogue, and it was closed up tight. So the cab driver took me to a lousy pizzeria near the Coliseum.

I drank a big bottle of aqua minerale con gas. It tasted too sulphury and seemed to make me even thirstier. I ate vegetable antipasto and vermicelli which looked more like fat worms than pasta. It almost made me gag but I ate it anyway because I was so hungry. A boy with glasses who I knew was American looked over a few times. He finally came over and told me he had seen me speak at Brown University recently and how much he liked me. I got up, forgetting the map David and Phillip had left me, and made the kid, whose name was Eric, walk me to the Coliseum.

It was all locked up but I spotted two kittens, dead to the world, asleep on top of a grate inside the gate. I knew they were probably disease-ridden but I loved looking at them all stretched out, snoozing. It was much more inspiring than staring at broken statues with only the feet remaining.

The kid was good company but he didn't save me from being accosted by three dirty, stupid Gypsy kids trying to pull their bent-cardboard trick. I screamed "Fuck off!" at them and gave them one of my really scary faces, but I have to admit it kind of scared me. I mean if I saw them sleeping inside the Coliseum like the kittens I would have thought they were sweet, but out on the street they weren't so damn precious.

We walked back to the hotel. I found a pharmacy open and purchased a loofa sponge. I mean, it's insane, but they don't provide washcloths in a four-star hotel in Rome—don't these people scrub themselves? With all this dirt and grime, I find it hard to believe.

I made dinner plans with Eric, then went to my room and slept again. It was beginning to bother me, all this sleep. I called Marilyn, the costume designer, who didn't sound that happy to hear from me. She must have been sleeping too, so who knows? We talked about having dinner, but I never heard back from her, which was fine because Moira called to invite me to a dinner party.

Eric and I went to the party after we had dinner at one of the restaurants we found last night. I remembered exactly how to get there, didn't miss a beat, right near the French embassy. The fish was good, and it was nice to be with Eric because I didn't feel like I had to impress him.

The party was a typical Italian scene. There was this big campy older actress of Bertolucci and Pasolini fame, Lara Betti, whom everyone grabbed and kissed—she didn't seem too thrilled about it.

I'm glad we ate elsewhere. I follow my instincts on these matters now; I can't wait until eleven to eat—I get horrible gas pains. And this way I wasn't obligated to stay forever and carry on that kind of conversation that drives me crazy. Like talking to this hyper English guy who knew me from *King of Comedy,* and this poseur bore from New York, Alan, who is obsessed with Warhol and sometimes wears his wig (Andy's), and who does horrible paintings, one of which he sold to some poor shmuck at the dinner. He was talking in my face, boring the shit out of me. Party talk was all about Almodovar. I started spacing out so we left.

Eric took off to his pensione so he wouldn't get locked out at midnight. I stopped at Hemingways, a bar as phony as its namesake. A cup of American coffee and tax, tap water posing poorly as aqua minerale, for twelve thousand lira. Oh well, it was like that all day today.

I am now back in my room after using the Bidet as usual and then freshening up after. I love being able to wash my butt after a long hot night.

Normally when I'm away from home for long periods of time I rarely think about my house. But for some reason, on a short weekend in Positano on a break from a long stay in Rome, visions of my place continually popped into my head. I thought about my new couch and the older one I'd left on the other side of the room across from it, and how cluttered and confused my living room seemed the day I left—a week ago. How much I would have liked coming home to a completed living room and dining area. But John thought I was crazy when I told him I wanted to find a new table right before leaving and maybe he was right. I could possibly be crazy but I wanted so much for everything to be perfect when I came home.

There were some nasty Italians working me on the walk back from the Spanish Steps this morning. This one guy, who had all the charm of Mussolini, was carrying a video recorder and laughing at me in a very childish, fucked-up way. I finally looked right at him and said "Grow up or die asshole!" It's a worldwide conspiracy of idiots and you can find them wherever you go. Well, we'll see how it all goes when Jackie descends on the scene— Bona sera darling . . . love love and love.

is what she called me last night lying in bed. It was bound to happen, only a matter of time.

She smoked a cigarette out on the balcony and then downed an airplane bottle of scotch. It surprised me; she recently changed drinks. It used to be Vodka, of course. Let's see if I can recount it all; I'd hate to miss even one nuance, but there were so many.

Yes, she was lying next to me with her eyes closed as if she'd recently married into royalty, some incredible princess. Now keep in mind we had just taken a road trip all around Tuscany and thought we had maybe for once worked out some of our irreconcilable differences. But give someone with a drinking problem a pack of Marlboros and a drink, and her problem becomes "ours."

"I love 2 Live Crew—they're what I'm about. (Oh really?) And Sinead O'Connor is great—I think she's the best."

"Yeah she is great." I reply in a monotone.

"But my religion is literary references. . . . (she's waiting for a response) . . . I've always loved Pucci."

"Uh huh."

"And sometimes I'll slap on just three drops of French perfume."

"That's all?" (I watch her working hard to get me to react.)

"You're a sexless American. You walk like a sexless American, you're rude and crass and everyone knows you're an American."

"What a horror."

"If I could seduce anybody in the world who would it be? Charles Sacchi, Larry Gogasian, Flea from the Red Hot Chili Peppers, Sean Young."

"You've always had good taste."

"I fucked Karl on the beach. We had alcohol poisoning and swam in the Santa Monica Bay and just fucked in the sand it got everywhere and it was very good and in the morning we fucked again and it was great and I told Paul, my 'brother,' about it and I was scared that I might fall in love with him but he was mean to me. . . . (I see the desperation in her eyes) . . . You know what? You make me sick, singing in that boutique in Florence. Who do you think you are? Barbara Streisand? Liza Minelli?"

"Correct me if I'm wrong, but wasn't I buying you an Armani sweater at the time?"

"Who cares? It was on sale, you cheap bitch. I knew this was a mistake wasting my money to come visit you in Rome. I'm leaving right now."

"Where are you going at three in the morning?"

"I'll sleep in the train station, maybe some cretin will rape me and then I can take the first train to Marion's villa where at least I'll be treated with some dignity."

"Oh really, you know something I don't?"

"Oh fuck you. Shut up, darling, or I'll break this bottle and cut my wrists."

"Great, then neither one of us will have to listen to your bullshit anymore."

"'Bye darling, I'm out the door, history, G-O-N-E!"

She was at the elevator when I finally decided to stop her.

"Thanks for picking up my spirits Jackie—I've had so much fun driving around Italy spending money on you and getting tortured."

She threw her hair back, ran her tongue over her lips, and as the elevator doors closed I watched her applying red lipstick in the mirror of her compact.

He had been away for a very long time, not that it was so unusual, but this had been a particularly rough job that took him to a former Eastern bloc country where, although things had changed some, it was quite dismal and lonely.

He made a great friend though, an English man with style and insight who brought him through the craziness they had both gotten themselves into; and despite the anxiety, they had a great time, like making the best of an unexpected stay in some lost world.

They became accustomed to each other and when goodbyes were said it was very sad, and he became apprehensive about going home again.

He arrived on Thanksgiving night so he missed the festivities and had the driver take him straight home. Exhaustion, confusion, disorientation were adjectives his mind played with all along the San Diego Freeway. Afraid to close his eyes, he watched the lights come up in the Valley. Of course traffic was light so he made it home very fast.

When he pulled into the driveway he immediately noticed that the porch light had burned out and that no one had bothered to replace it; this upset him and he swore under his breath and felt his heart with the palm of his hand. The driver sensed his anxiousness and helped him in with the luggage.

When he turned the key and opened the door two things struck him very deeply: the alarm did not go off, and she was sitting on his brand new brocade couch smoking and burning holes in the fabric. She looked up with the coldest of smiles and waited for a reaction.

Ceasar made the curtains in my living room. I waited a very long time for them as he had an unfortunate experience from which he barely escaped. Steven told me that some blood splattered on one of the panels and I began to question the karma of these curtains that were to hang proudly in my home which I had avoided decorating for close to five years.

Ceasar was recovering slowly back in New York with his mother, to whom he was incredibly close. He seemed frail when I first met him out in L.A. Having dressed store windows in Manhattan, he came to get away from the pressures of the big city. He was wonderfully imaginative.

He called me a few months after this terrible encounter he had with a drugged-out midnight cowboy, who lost his mind and tried to kill him. He told me the story with great restraint and a humor that impressed me. But he was a man of his word and was indeed finishing my beautiful drapes.

Several weeks later he made the trek back to L.A. to hang them. It took a good part of the day. He ironed them tenderly, the rich iridescent purple taffeta backed by a yellowish gold lining, all interwoven along the top with gold braid. He sat on top of a ladder, tying knots, explaining the theatricality he hoped to achieve with the fabric he chose and the way they hung. They transformed my house and I could see it was a triumph for him.

He went back to New York where I later saw him with a man who made rugs. He seemed in good spirits and planned on coming out in September to finish up the house for me, odds and ends and such. The summer disappeared and it was early August when I heard he was doing poorly over at Sloan Kettering, a name I fear thinking of, let alone saying out loud. I spoke to his Mom on a Saturday afternoon and she wasn't doing well herself. We spoke quietly, as if I were close enough to whisper in her ear. I heard in her voice the guilt and tragic tone of someone letting go.

It was only two hours later that she called to say he was gone. She held in all the terror, and then released it, telling me how proud Ceasar was to have made those curtains for me, that it had really meant a lot to him to finish the job. Thank you, she said, for giving that to him. I told her to call me if there was anything I could possibly do.

When I hung up the phone I was struck with the thought that it is always the mothers who suffer the most, that they are there when the mortal suffering ends, and it is they who carry the torch of sweet sons, dear friends. It dawned on me I'd been seeing a lot of mothers holding up quite proudly these days, and I invited all of them to accept my deep regard and love, for there is little else I have to offer.

There are tombstone benches at the bus stops in West Hollywood. I wonder what they are trying to tell us as I drive past. Are they aimed at the old people who wait for the RTD to drive them down Fairfax to buy a loaf of challah or a nice piece of kosher beef? Or for the gay boys who ponder their mortality, blinded by the sun as they gaze at billboards offering home care for the unmentionable disease? Was it just a design oversight or an intentional fond farewell to all those who disturb the horizon along Santa Monica, all those fragile souls buying cartons of orange juice and things that go down easy at the Alpha Beta? Maybe those benches whisper, "Move along people, get on the buses and disappear." I don't like them, however they are meant to be interpreted. They depress me and I wish someone would take them away.

It was going to be the last time I did this to myself. I was lying on my bed, eyes closed. The drilling out on the street was a comfort compared to what I was putting myself through. And I just wanted to at least *think* this could possibly be the last time anyway.

There are tortures that come in varying shades of pain and remorse. I specialize in the big "set up," as it were. I am great at seduction and have gone to incredible lengths to get someone if I really want them. There is faxing, FedExing (at others' expense), endless sexy, graphic letters accompanied by incredible homemade tapes of exotic imports. There is always great preparation and frequent glances in the mirror to be sure a bang has not fallen to the wrong side, or that under-eye cover hasn't faded, casting dark circles in bad light; there is the change, and the right combination of perfumes, and all this just to write the damn letter let alone actually see this person in the flesh. I am spoiled and angry when things do not go my way immediately.

I can barely focus during dinners. There is a dreamscape around me, misty, blurry, unrelenting; our knees touch under the table, there is a lingering connection between the eyes.

"Oh honey, we have to find someone to take care of you!"

I smile that shy "but it really has to be you" smile. And then, perhaps a segue that is seemingly a non sequitur into a discussion of lovers I've peed on—just for a reaction.

"Oh, it's very *Story of the Eye,* isn't it?"

Hurry, hurry, maybe something futile and terribly, tragically romantic is awaiting us back at the hotel (these encounters only happen when away from home).

But when you get there they suddenly remember having to meet up with some visiting German fashion designer, and they leave you to face the fact you once again gave too much to the wrong person.

If you only knew, maybe someday you will, that I only ever loved you and cared deeply about what had been done to you, the childhood love you never knew, the abandonment of adults too involved with their own earthly desires to notice how fragile you truly were, and still are, even more now than then. I watched so I know, I listened. It resonates still, in my dreams at night and my heart when I hear some sad little melody that reminds me of you, when you weren't striking out or building those lonely walls I could no longer break down, for I had sadness of my own and always will. But in spite of everything you imagine to be cruel and spoiled about the love we once had, I cradle it in my prayers and best wishes for all that you are and could be.

Okay, this is sick, pre–Rosh Hashana perversity. If I could send a really honest birthday greeting to her this is what it would be:

Dear _____ ,

What kind of birthday are you having, is it a *gas?* Are you sucking cock or eating pussy? What's the drink for the day? Maybe martinis with a champagne chaser—or are you sipping wine and then some scotch? After all, we are moving into cooler weather. Oh darling, is someone absolutely sweeping you off your gnarly feet? Some dashing dowager with loads of cold cash and hot cum? Are you wearing blue eye-liner and something Sly and the Family Stone? Or are you all Coco'd up to the twat and poured into Pucci?!! Tights and headbands, old stinking Gigli flats, the tackiest Gucci belt just dripping with fake gold coins? Are you sitting in that ensemble reading Montaigne or Sarte? Have you reached the point with your new lover in purple neon where you uncontrol-lably attack him at 2:00 A.M. or are you still in the stage of awe?

Do you slide into his Mercedes and coyly light a Marlboro, gently insert a 2 Live Crew CD and blast it, simulating an erotic Prince-like, Vanity-style dance on his warm leather seat? Does your ultra wet oozing cunt leave a ring of exquisite cherry juice on the upholstery? Do you reach over and caress his thigh, perching precariously near his ever-hardening prick? Do you unzip his fly, oooooo, the sound sends shivers down your arching back, and pull his pink lollipop out of its panties? Did you make him wear purple lace girlie panties so you can seduce him, shoving three fingers up his pulsating sphincter? Do you rub the head of his cock like a genie's Aladdin Vegas lamp, rub a dub dub out pour the silver dollars for our pretty princess? Everybody loves a winner!!!

Do you casually mention how you always wanted—dreamed of—being a forties star? Does he swerve on Mulholland, terrifying your beauty? Do you throw back your long gorgeous mane of hair held in place by a Pucci headband? How original, but then you always loved Pucci. Do you throw back your head revealing nicotine, espresso-stained bottom teeth? It does make the fronts look so white, like great back lighting!! Are you wrapped in a fun fur like dear dear Lara from *Dr. Zhivago* riding through this cold night in a buggy to your dasha?

Do you tell him controversial asides like how you

are terrified of getting old and how much you hate fat people and old people, or isn't it quite time for anything that intense? After all, it is your birthday and he sent you the most gorgeous roses ever and you can't help but notice that huge bag from Chanel sliding around the back seat. Not unlike your hand on his ever-growing prick. Murmurs of the heart, baby, oh this is love for certain, big love, David Lynch—directed love, Nick Cage/Laura Dern love, emphasis on smelly cigarette heads not unlike the tip of your man's exploding red penis. Oh baby, does it hurt? you ask him with such feeling, because my pussy is in agony right now, oh let's swing into some cheap motel, maybe someone like Willem Dafoe will be there and try to fuck me but then you'll save me. Oh darling, I'm so so deliciously, deliriously happy on my birthday. You are heaven, darling and I'm just dying for a martini and some heroin!! Just kidding on the H!!

I'm so bad for you but I need the refuge of your perfect arms to hold me when I feel for certain that I might be going insane. You have to sleep with me every night. I can't stand to be alone. No one should be ever be. Life is all about seduction and great fucking. I want to strap on a dildo and fuck your ass so hard you lose consciousness. I just adore futile anal sex!! Oh sweetheart, I can't believe it, you got us a suite at the Bel Air! I'm so completely mad about you, but who will see us here? Only joking Darling!!! This is heaven, oh God, a new Chanel bag!! I'm absolutely going to faint—this is it darling, I'm yours forever, marry me. Happy birthday to me, this is the ultimate Marxist experience, oh fuck me darling right now!! This is the perfect martini!!

oh darling,
do have the happiest Birthday ever
and know I love you!!!

Did I tell you I've been cooking again? I'm really turning my house into a home. Isn't it just strange and wonderful when you stop longing for everything Out There to make you okay in here? I tell you there's nothing like stuffing pieces of garlic into a Rocky Junior, you know, one of those free range chickens from Mrs. Gooch's. When the heat pours out of the oven and I baste the browning bird with all those good juices, it makes me never want to read another issue of *Vanity Fair*. I mean could the Sotheby's auction of Princess Gloria's inherited jewels ever compete with the sound or smell of a sizzling potato browning in a big iron skillet? Could the murder involving a sociopathic hustler measure up to a chocolate soufflé rising majestically? Maybe all that glamour has worn me out, perhaps I've caused one too many scenes, danced away all my lost weekends, but I just don't think I'll be joining you this time.

I miss Daniel today. It has been almost a year since we said goodbye. I kissed both of his hands—he had the most beautiful hands, long, supple fingers. I asked him if I had disappointed him all those years ago when I didn't love him the way he loved me. I kept think-ing that if only we had gotten together he wouldn't be dying now. He said of course not, but when I got back to L.A. we talked on the phone and he told me, crying hard, that he had been just a young boy and I was the most beautiful woman he had ever known. We talked two or three times a day that week. He was so clear and I made him laugh a lot, I felt good about that, but it was obvious he wasn't getting better. The last time I heard his voice he was pretty incoherent with a terrible fever. It was one of those horrible moments when you expect crying in the background. And all of those questions run through your head. What do we do now? Sell his house? Who gets his things? Gives the talks? Reminiscences? Do you mourn now or wait, and try to hold on to the memory of his last breath?

I lit candles and a fire and hoped he sensed that all of this, that his life had not been for nothing. I prayed for that more than anything, prayed that the transition was gentle and pure, not unlike his life.

So here I sit, in Budapest, gray, cold, almost a year later not knowing quite what to make of the passage of time. Time that brought people into and out of my life in different ways. Some with spirits reminiscent of Daniel's, irrepressible and ecstatic, who continue in the tradition of total honesty and love Daniel and I had. Those who understand too, who soothe me without ever knowing how deeply I need it.

Every night I say prayers for Daniel just so he knows that when my day ends and I'm ready to dream he will always be one of the last waking thoughts I have and perhaps one of the first dreams of my sleeping night.

A child's voice woke me in the strange night. The train was weaving in and out of mountain passes and I couldn't sleep in the tiny bunk. She was whispering to her mother in some secret language that I could only sense.

Her mother stroked her forehead but never smiled during the many hours I observed them that day. Her husband sat next to me smoking cigarettes with a filter. One would have never guessed they knew each another since he never so much as glanced over at them or showed any signs of caring at all.

I sat across from them at dinner. The child looked sickly and frightened and the father kept smiling at me when he thought they weren't looking. He was very handsome and I felt guilty for engaging him at all. They finally left the dining car, which was a relief, but then I saw them again going into their cabin.

I had booked only a single, and it was next to them. I was trying several positions to get comfortable and heard the mother singing a lullaby, the soft murmuring of the little girl. They fell quiet sometime later while I managed to count backward from a hundred and drift off.

I was awakened by the loud angry voice of the man who

was accusing the woman of giving all her attention to that "little rat, dirty sick worm." And how there were hundreds of women who could give him the love he deserved. She was crying and the child awoke. All of us were up together until someone screamed at them to shut up, that "this wasn't a tenement, we are not traveling second class, go ride with the commoners."

This seemed to calm everyone down. The man closed the door, I heard him smoking and breathing in the aisle, and the whispering voice of the little girl lulled me back to my dreaming.

I had never seen faces like the ones staring out at me from a parallel train driving into Budapest. Exhausted and empty I had left everyone else behind, some had been drinking too much and were now throwing up while waiting for their luggage.

But these faces racing by me, silhouetted and shadowed, looking outward onto concrete chalets painted in grim shades of green, beige, and mauve. Already the winter sky was creeping in, little smoldering piles burned outside in factory fields. Shacks, industry, unfinished roads, miles of railroad track leading nowhere, endlessly twisting and turning through a million lives.

An ambiguous old man wearing a peaked cap walks in a field which runs along side the highway. Hands folded behind his back, he's moving as slowly as the cars on the highway. People on a tennis court, the grayest of apartment buildings, ancient automobiles billowing out leaded fumes, while drivers with stained yellow fingers puff on unfiltered cigarettes. I have arrived in Budapest.

Where does the time go? In minutes the months grace us with old thoughts, tender times. I remember rubbing your neck and wondering how it really made you feel, kissing you on the cheek as the lights went to black (amazed at my own confidence). I could've loved you a million times but I never let myself, so these feelings continue to well up in me still from time to time.

I'm nervous to see you, if it's tonight or sometime soon. I think about looking at you from across the table, wanting to reach out and hold your face in my hands, wishing you were just like my dreams, soft, forgiving, the characteristics I long to impose on you—how can anyone live up to them?

Smoke whirls all around me, smoke that doesn't belong to me, that I had no hand in creating. It is blown in my face over dinners in London, back over a cab driver's shoulder in Rome, from some girl's Gauloise on the Metro in Paris, on international first-class Swiss Air flights while stuck next to a chic man from Bombay. An endless cloud of smoke whispers in my ear, hangs around my head like a victorious garland, rests mysteriously in a lover's kiss. A match strikes up and the tip of another cigarette swells with mad passion. There it is next to me in my own bed, smoke following me into dreams and over morning coffee, hanging, haunting, driving me completely insane. A well-meaning admirer blows smoke up my ass. A brief respite as I blow it back into the face it came from, I take it personally, like a big fuck you. My clothes go directly into the hamper where they sit and stew and stink as I pass them by the morning after.

In launderettes in London they smoke while they wash.

A woman with very damaged blonde hair and as much ambition as she could muster, put a load of dingy whites and lackluster colors all together in an ugly round white machine.

"What does that do?" I asked.

"Oh, it's a spinner. Takes out the extra water so it's cheaper to dry them."

I couldn't take my eyes off that contraption.

An older woman wears flowered mules that scrape across the launderette floor. She takes out a huge load from the washer and keeps moving her false teeth back and forth habitually. She picks up a nearly smoked-up butt from the top of the washer, takes a few more puffs and flicks it out the door. Her laundry basket rests in a baby stroller, all the white and colors together, a huge burden blended into one.

She pauses, looks across to the blonde. "That's it for another week, then." Her slip hangs down below the hem of her dress in slight tatters. She waves to the washer woman. "'Bye, Mary, see you next time."

Her mouth is inverted as she winks goodbye. She did not use the dryer.

A man, smoking, drinking a Coke, and reading a novel of international intrigue helps me secure the door of the big washer. And as water pours out of the smaller one where I did my whites, he closes that door tightly for me as well. He does it without any trace of condescension or irritation for which I am thankful, because it feels so nice to be in London where I can listen in on the blonde woman and her older friend with the tattered slip hanging down. It seems like everyone's clothes are slowly falling apart.

I quickly throw my clothes into the dryer before they absorb the smell of smoke and I have to wash them again.

A woman walks in looking very butch, wearing a tight black stretch skirt with a dirty off white cable sweater. She's the mother of the two mixed babies. It seems almost as if she is babysitting them, as if the color of their skin makes them strangers even to her. She is white and flat with an alienlike featureless face; the babies have character only by the blackness of them. She's lucky, the father must be good looking, so at least she's had something of beauty in her life. But maybe it confuses her, too rich for her blood.

The blonde is back with her redheaded daughter and her friend in green sweatshorts who waits quietly outside with her arms folded.

A Chinese woman puts in a load. Next to me the machine starts gushing water but the proprietor, an Indian man, touches the door lightly in just the right place and it stops.

Mary the washerwoman mops it up, as she did for me, and the Chinese woman declares "It was magic when he touched the machine."

No one responds, except for a smile, maybe.

The owner's wife comes in smoking and smartly dressed, with a tight perm. Her little girl has a dustpan and brush and wants to sweep the floor. Mary and another white woman in a colorful print dress fold big yellow sheets, and the fat little Indian girl wants to help. The wife blows smoke in my face. While holding the mixed baby, the blonde and redheaded daughter fold another load.

A girl of fifteen or so comes in looking for her mother. She opens the dryer and recognizes the clothes so she knows her mother is around. The washerwoman holds the mixed babies, so cute and soft.

I put all my wet laundry in the dryer, colors and whites together. It feels great seeing how white my underpants are again.

I never wash anything but tender bras by hand, but for weeks in Rome I'd been washing everything out in the sink and letting them dry on the balcony. Nothing smelled good or fresh. Walking around Rome I always felt dirty, incomplete.

I'm lying on the bed thinking of home where I can do a small load if I need a pair of jeans or just want to freshen up some towels.

Nina sits like a statue in the Musee d'Orsay, like a vision, kismet, a dream. She is wearing a coat made of endangered species: python, leopard, mink. But as she, too, is on the verge of extinction, there is no love lost between these beasts of burden.

The rude French guard tells the great lady she must abandon her throne; she casts him a glance that could destroy a kingdom, let alone this serf. But she rises majestically and summons John and I out to the street. She is extremely hungry and would like to take lunch at Angelina's Tea Room. We move the entourage into a taxi, Nina Simone in Paris, how inspiring.

We sit for hours. She eats well, her coat hangs by itself near our table. I stare at it while listening to endless stories about the years that have passed, some grand, others disasters.

"They stole my Porgy money," she belts out. "The rock jabbers, thieves. I had all the cards stacked against me: I'm black, I'm a woman, I'm beautiful, and as if that wasn't enough, on top of that I'm talented too!"

She enjoyed her foie gras, John and I paid the check— great talents do not carry money, it is much too crass. We tell her we've been to the Virgin record store on Champ Elysees and that they have even her most obscure albums.

"I want to see for myself. Let's go," she tells us in a voice that all at once seems to go from deep southern to Liberian. And we are off again.

At Virgin she wants to see records of sales, how many orders for her CDs, but they refuse to show her. Although Paris is her city, there seems to be some resistance this day.

"Put these CDs in your bag," she says to her assistant. "They told me it was fine to take them. After all, they belong to me." Her assistant humors her, not wanting to cause a further scene. Nina says do what I say. John tries to calm her down. I am so exhausted I walk back to my hotel for a nap.

Along the way I am humming a beautiful melody, "Fodder On My Wings," and remembering the time I waited for Nina to come out and sing at the Vine St. Bar and Grill. When she finally came on she asked everyone in the audience to give her fifteen dollars to make up for her missing "Porgy money." Some people left but I didn't mind. She sang so sadly that I stayed for her late set as well.

I thought about her in Paris today and how hard it was to tell her I adored her. Perhaps it would have been best to let her sit comfortably in the Musee d'Orsay and be admired from a distance.

Who knew when I accepted the invitation to be in the Commes Des Garcons show in Paris last March that I was to meet the love of my life. How strange and beautiful to see this incredible woman-child sitting on the floor next to a rack of black strapless dresses, so calm and sad in the midst of all this high-couture attitude. She drew me in, and I turned to Ada and said "Look at this girl. She is the most wonderful thing I've ever seen. I have to have her." I kept staring at her and when she finally looked up and noticed me, I embarrassedly responded "Oh, I'm sorry I keep staring, but I'm really out of it. I'm starving—as a matter of fact I was thinking of eating you." She laughed so I figured she got it, only to discover later she had no idea what the hell I was talking about—English is her third language.

Of course I fell in love with her immediately when she told me about the Indians in the Amazon and how the only thing they wanted was love and she would like to take me there.

When do we leave, I asked.

The show was so magical, all Marianne Faithfull's haunting music, and by the end of it I was riveted to

Gabriella. I told her to meet me at my hotel that afternoon. She had saved two glasses of champagne for us after the show—we drank them and then she left suddenly. I knew she would forget the name of the hotel, so I had Ada track her down at a fitting. She came over forty-five minutes later, bringing pastries which I ate as I caressed her arm and gently persuaded her to kiss me, which she did quite incredibly. We had Indian food for dinner, she stayed with me that night and I haven't stopped thinking of her since.

It was a night that did not threaten or remind me of anything I'd ever felt before. There was the promise of a distant thunderstorm and the memory of what we'd done and a sense that life always continues all around us in its constant, quiet way with no one, no amount of power able to interrupt its flow. I was awed and thoughtful the entire way home.

When I got inside, your presence had all but disappeared. A blanket you left behind had gathered dust on the closet floor and I was afraid to touch it, so I sat for quite some time on the edge of the guest bed (still made up in green flannel), pondering how you had intentionally scattered bits of memory all around my house, knowing that I'd come home to it and it would sadden me, tear me up in some way.

I figured that romance must be put on hold with you out of reach and all this craziness that I was constantly sweeping out of my house and out of my life. I had to discipline myself to not jump into the next set of strange arms. You were so completely in control; choosing to crush me or inspire me, until I woke up one morning and took back the power that had always been mine—then I could laugh at your cruelty and I wasn't a victim anymore. Sometimes I lay in bed on those cold winter sheets and I stay in one spot and recall all the wonderful times we had—and sometimes I feel as if I can barely remember you at all.

I always felt that I could collapse and you'd pull me back up in your rescuer's arms; I guess it was my projection but what a beautiful fantasy, one I wish had come true, my needs so deep. How could anyone protect me from the reality I saw so clearly and at the same time chose to ignore? You were beautiful as my fantasy; no one ever looked at me the way you did, and that was something I could never really get over (being such a daydreamer).

No one can ever fall so far without breaking her heart.

"I swear to you I didn't try to kiss her," he said, but his mother slapped him across the face anyway. He sat stunned for the moment, very still, his plate of dinner growing colder by the minute. Everything now seemed pointless, he thought, really no way to make sense of any of this. He asked to be excused, his father nodded, and he got up from the table. She looked up at him and saw how strong he'd become and she loved him for that.

He walked lightly down the hallway groping the wall into his room, closing the door quietly behind him, something he always did—force of habit from coming in late from work and clubs.

Some nights he barely made it to his bed thinking of her beauty. He knew his mother was right, she was distant and different from him. But when they had long talks she let her guard down so they could be close and hold each other. They already knew that time would drag them down long and separate roads, and this moved them.

Night faded as he dropped her down the block and watched as she disappeared into her own house, far away from anything he had ever known. Sometimes he would cry all the way home, biting the inside of his cheek, the cold stinging his ears and blistering his soft lips.

A part of him always stayed behind with her as she thought about his lonely walk home and everything they had told each other on this night and all the others. But nothing seemed as heavy as his own thoughts and she knew that too. That's why he loved her.

He locked his door tonight, not because it mattered but as a gesture of complete solitude. He heard his parents talking in the living room, it pleased him that perhaps they might be speaking about him. He put a record on the stereo, a Bach Concerto, and began reading a book of poems. After some time he got up and stood by his window, watching a gentle rain fall. He stuck his face out the open window and let the water run over him, closed his eyes and let all his deepest hurt go running on to the grass below.

Whipping winds bent back the trees and knocked him off balance and he knew nothing could ever stop him again, not a slap across his face, not all the years that would separate him from lovers and dear friends, not even the fear of losing all sense of himself. The rain washed this away and the wind carried it over the trees and forgiving earth.

He watched as lights went out here and there; people were going to sleep now. He sensed a great change too, and through the bedroom door, closed and locked with utmost care, his father said goodnight and something else he chose to believe he heard: I love you.

Carefully he closed the window. Drawing the shade, he laid down and remembered as much as he could before drifting to sleep, knowing that in the morning the change, already a part of his daily routine, would be forgotten, and he slept quite well.

"I just wanted you to be proud of me," she said, tears running down her face, snot hanging out of her nose. "To love me like you love your success, your fame, your money and everything it bought you: unconditional love and respect."

She threw herself down on the bathroom floor, cold, black, water drenched. First on her stomach and then on her back, feeling a cold coming on, coughing and letting the spit squish between the tile and her cheek. If she could have bled she would, but she had no strength to cut herself nor the courage to ask him to do it for her.

He sat like an emperor on the toilet seat, closed and shiny. Looking down on her with judgment, without pity, frozen in detachment, longing to be anywhere but with her losing it, self-destructive, lost.

"When are you going to get up and blow your nose? I can't talk to you like this. I can't love you or blame myself when I see you collapsing right here in front of me."

She got up on her knees, which was no small feat, since she'd bruised them badly when she threw herself down on the floor. And she went to him, puffed up, swollen, a bundle of jangled nerves and good intentions.

_____

"I need your approval, make me beautiful, take me in front of your fabulous friends and tell them I matter, that I make a difference in your world."

She hugged his knees knowing she would hate him in fifteen minutes, once she got a grip on herself. But in that moment, just the touch of his hands, the gold ring cold on her forehead, soothed her, cooled her dark hell.

The future did not figure into this desperate, hateful scene of lust and instant gratification. No, nothing really mattered except the short walk into the bedroom, lights dimmed, cold drafts chilling her on white sheets, caresses that postpone decisions, kisses that mangle lips and thighs, new and silent releases of ancient fears and regrets. This is all that concerned them, the relentless forgiveness of love.

There were gruesome scenes before but this one took the cake. When she looked out her window early that summer morning, there were four cop cars and two ambulances surrounding the bungalows on Havenhurst. The stretchers, covered in sheets, held the bodies of two people she barely knew who had acknowledged her at least a hundred times. Watching their bodies being carried out, she wished she had known them better.

They had always seemed so interesting, the man and the woman, the man, constantly clad in a fedora and a large overcoat, even on the hottest of Los Angeles days, those days when the sun blazed and broke sweat even in the quiet curtain-drawn living rooms of so many anonymous people who were living in the midst of a proud war, a war that bonded the oddest people through rationing, nylon hose, lady riveters, high hopes.

This was not a vision she wanted to greet early on a Monday morning on her way to work as a bank teller, where her busy days were spent cashing modest checks for older gentlemen and perky girls.

She could recall the woman pausing by the fountain to adjust the seam in her hose. She remembered staring at her, but the woman, oblivious to scrutiny, kept straightening her seam and smiling, confidently. She remembered it like a Norman Rockwell painting, a scene from American life waiting to be snuffed out without rhyme or reason and she regretted that she hadn't said hello, how are you, to her. The woman could only respond instinctively to her very intense stare, a stare that couldn't be broken even by her own nervous laughter. But the woman heard her and laughed back in acknowledgment of her fear and confusion.

She would spend much of her time in restaurants, using her limited salary on blue plate specials laced with heavy gravies and canned green beans. She had a penchant for lettuce salads; at restaurants like Musso and Frank's she would sit alone at the counter, light up a smoke, have a cup of coffee and a piece of cake for dessert, fold her newspaper carefully under her arm. She always carried her umbrella in hopes it would rain.

She remembered seeing the couple behind a sheer curtain dancing in very slow rhythmic movements, she watched for a long time, perhaps too long, and wondered, but she never knocked on their door and asked "Can I come in, can I watch, pour myself a cognac, a scotch?"

Sometimes she saw them sitting out on their porch drinking tall, cool, frosty drinks, the kind that only the very indulgent and very confident would sip so blatantly out in the middle of a communal courtyard in West Hollywood. But right now, their dreams, their dancing, their cool confident drinking all came to a screeching halt on a bright, piercing Monday morning, a hot and very distant angry Monday morning in Los Angeles.

The police carried out the odd-shaped bags, the sheets over their faces making an outline of noses and mouths. Other people watched from behind curtains, sun-bleached and frayed. Some men in suspenders and bare chests stood chewing on cigars, appraising the situation with the arrogance of the very smug, shuffling back and forth in old house slippers. Raucous laughter filled the courtyard, nasty innuendos of what might have happened at 1046½ last night.

The police questioned everyone around, bringing those smirks to an end, before they knocked on her door. A great big burly cop twice her age rapped on the door and she answered promptly.

"What can I do sir, what can I do for you officer?"

"Well, there's been a problem."

"Yeah, I can see that."

"Maybe you can shed some light on it probably happened around four thirty A.M. Ya hear anything?"

"No sir, wish I had, I was sound asleep, tossing and turning a little bit."

"Oh, maybe you felt something going on."

"Maybe, maybe I did, I don't acknowledge those things though."

"Well it's better not to sometimes. Haven't seen any-body suspicious around here?"

"Everybody's suspicious officer, everybody in this world.

"It's true, we're living in suspicious times. Could be a commie, a Nazi, a Jap."

"Yeah, or it could just be an actor or a bank teller."

"Yeah, you got a good sense of humor lady. Mind if I look around?"

"Well, there's nothing really to look at in my place."

"Yeah, you're probably right, just routine, just checkin', you bein' right across from them and everything."

"Sure, you can come in." She let him into her small apartment, ushered him into the dark living room.

"Want some orange juice, a cup of coffee?"

"Oh no, no thanks we gotta get movin'. Got other places to go, other murders to solve, other nameless faces to slap a name on."

"Well, good luck. You got ninety percent of this town to do that to officer. You got a big job ahead of you."

"That's what I look forward to, big jobs in a little town."

"This ain't no little town."

"Oh, to me it is. It's just a little town, a sad sleepy town that got too big for its britches. I like to kick it in the butt sometimes, calm it down."

"Well, officer I'm glad you're out there. We need more men like you—straightforward, always sure of what you want and not afraid to get it. Wish I knew what want or who I wanted."

"Gee, lady you sound like you're lost. This could be the wrong town for a girl like you. You an actress or somethin'?"

"Oh, I'm always acting, I'm acting out my whole life, acting out a scene no matter where I am."

"Well lady I'd like to get a big earful from you but I gotta to move on. I got real mysteries to solve, kids crying out there who lost their parents, wives hanging over their husbands with steaks knives at their chests. I seen it all lady, I seen the husbands kill the wives, wives kill the girlfriends. I've seen kids ready to lose their minds, had to put them in homes, separate families, that's how it all ends sometimes, you know."

"Oh officer it sounds so romantic. I wish I could go with you and see it, even that sight, going into the ambulance seems more enticing than anything I've ever known."

"Lady you got some crazy notion about glamour, but you're in the right town I guess. Little town jam-packed with excitement. God knows, glamour hits new lows in Hollywood."

"Yeah officer, I've been there, I'll be there again."

"Well, thanks very much ma'am. We'll be back in touch with you though, so I guess the thrill isn't over yet. We'll be questioning everybody around here for a while until we solve this damn thing."

"Officer, before you leave, what was the murder weapon?"

"Oh, huh, can't reveal that, can't reveal that. Gruesome sight though, not one of the more gruesome sights, but on a scale of one to ten, around a five, five and a half. I've seen it all lady. This one didn't shake me up, just brushed me, like a tumbleweed in the desert, blows past your leg, you feel it, but you let it keep going, you keep your eyes out for something much more dangerous, like a rattler. Can't stop to check out every tumbleweed, you know, every emotion just lasts an instant around here."

"Oh officer, I wish it lasted that long."

She closed the door after him, picked up her shiny new umbrella, because she was sure it would rain today, and walked out into the steamy California morning.

Jackie told me out of the blue as if it would come as some big shock and revelation that she got into a car wreck Wednesday night.

"Oh really, what happened?"

"Some drug addicts were running across the road (takes one to know one), so the woman in front of me slammed on her brakes and I didn't so I hit her."

"Did you tell her you didn't have any insurance?"

"No, we exchanged numbers and hopefully everything will be okay."

"Did you hurt your neck?"

"No."

"Well, it sounds like you just bumped into somebody."

"Well, it was a week of car wrecks."

"I'm sure this week will be better."

"Yes, well, that's how these things go." She paused, probably inhaling a cigarette. "You know I almost died last night."

"Oh really, I don't think it was quite that serious. Did you call your doctor today?"

"No, I've been too busy."

"What did your therapist say?"

"That I have a broken wing and I wasn't doing a very good job of mending myself, and I wasn't surrounded by very many people who are any good for me."

"How many sleeping pills did you take?"

"None last night."

"No, the night before?"

"Oh . . . three."

"What kind?"

"Halcyon, Adavan, and some French thing."

"What did your therapist say about that?"

"That I better be careful or I could die."

"That's the best she could come up with? That's really insightful."

"I had lunch at the Border Grill—it was awful!"

"What did you have?"

"Fish—echhh!"

"Yeah, it's not very good there. Who did you have lunch with?"

"My friend Thadius the professor."

"Did you ask him to renew your membership at the gym?"

"Yes. He said Joey, my trainer, missed me and I should come back. I said I would when I got myself out of debt. We decided I'm the least motivated person we know."

"Oh, is that true?"

"Not really, I meant to ask him for a loan but I'm too

chicken. Well I should clean up and do laundry but I haven't got the courage!"

"Well, summon it up and get it together and get some sleep."

"Are you angry at me?"

"Why would I be angry at you?"

"Your voice sounds angry at me."

"No. Everything is fine. I've got to go."

"You are mad at me."

"No, I'm not. I'll speak to you soon."

"Alright. Well, have fun."

Everything about her was remarkable. The way she walked with a conscious effort for femininity, her old Chanel bag constantly hanging on her elbow. Like Tippi Hedren in *The Birds,* they could have pecked her eyes out, but that damn bag would still be over her arm, perfectly positioned so she could calmly remove a cigarette and light it without effort or emotion. Her lipstick was perfect, always within the framework of the pencil lining them, full and lustrous—what Barbara Hershey tried to achieve with collagen.

Everything was taken for granted, reminding one of where she came from and who she had known. The way she left footprints in dust and greasy smears on bus windows, writing in a diary or changing her hose in a public restroom, throwing out old flowers and stale crackers.

Manny is a putz and that's all there is to it. It's not open for discussion so I don't want to hear anymore about it! He drove everyone in Vegas nuts, right out of their skulls, and this is on top of the fact that people bent over backwards for him. I mean busted their balls to make things nice. Smoothed ruffled feathers of guys who could have just pointed a finger at him and had him crushed into a zillion pieces. Made bad deals right, someone always driving out to the desert to take care of his fuckups. But it was never enough for our Manny. Emanuel Swartz with that gorgeous head of curly black hair, big, thick red lips and the body of Adonis!

I know Manny. I knew him better back then, when, according to reliable sources, I was a bit of a knockout myself. I didn't need anyone, and baby, that has its appeal. I mean I'd sit down at a blackjack table at the Dunes or the Sands and I'd buy a stack of chips and keep building it all night long. Sure I came from money but I never used people. And I never took my money for granted, or expected it to just rain down on my head.

I'd walk through the casinos in some killer strapless sequin number with my tits pushed up right under my chin, and forget Manny, every eye in the place, including schleppers from Ohio feeding the dime slots and high rollers from Texas with custom-made Stetsons and big diamond-studded gold watches, was on me. They would all pop up like a jack-in-the-boxes and shake their heads in sheer amazement at my ass alone.

I spent a lot of time with Manny and put up with his shit. Coming home in the middle of the night stinking drunk, pissing on the side of the toilet all over my fluffy seat cover. That was nothing of course, but it stuck in my craw.

When it came time to calling a spade a spade, my dad called me up to his office at the Flamingo, set down his scotch and water, took a puff on a fresh Havana cigar, and held my hands while making the "I love my little girl" proclamation. I requested that he cut to the chase and not wear his little girl's ass out.

"Honey, Manny's got to go. To be frank he's, well, on his way to disappearing permanently. I've talked and double talked on his behalf, but I can't have that two bit greasy little shit fucking up the business or my angel. Hey, what can I say, you're my baby and so pretty, I worry."

"Hey daddy, you could have phoned this one in. I'm late for my manicure."

"I like to tell you these things face to face. Call mommy would you?"

I left in a spoiled rotten little snit, went right out for a smoke, a long, tall, cool drink, and a dip in the pool. That big, tough, Nevada sun baking my bones felt damn good. I checked out some young stupid guys and tried to forget Manny, his initial pinky ring, and all the late mornings he'd screw me into heaven. So what if he wasn't the first, no doubt not the last, but I'm a sentimental broad with a soft spot for those brainless schmucks that Vegas breeds like so many chickens. Who cares—I love this town. I'm no lover but I sure hope Manny's gonna be okay.

When I left her as I was forced to do it was with constant self-examination and remorse, which I despised. Why was it necessary? I mean it wasn't like it hadn't happened at least twenty times already. I wanted to believe in her greatness or at least that quality I created and imbued her with. I remember opening my door at the Kensington Hilton, the nervousness in that tiny cozy room, her sitting in the chair and me on the edge of the bed perched like some terrified creature. She always seemed cold or detached when we got back together and it always left the ball in my court, which of course I'm used to (and have even been known to cultivate, but at this point would be more than happy to accommodate someone else's sense of duty and seduction).

Well, we went to dinner to Mr. Chow's with John and it was delicious and we walked back in the cold. We lit some candles and fucked and kissed and completely surrendered and I loved her like a stranger, without regret and with total compassion. I swore it was going to last forever although there was little if any reality ever between us, but I guess that's what I really responded to—the sheer madness and lust of it all. Yes she is beautiful in her way, but I feel our love is not pure or original and that saddens me still as I try to avoid it now and not reach for the phone. I can't take the insults anymore, but I am always willing to accept the tenderness of the touch.

Whenever I hear rap I get crazy with jealousy. I can see her dancing with some guy doing her funny mock-boxing maneuvers all jaunty with a ciggy hanging off the corner of her Chanel-red lips, swinging that ton of hair back and forth, and so willing and eager to give herself to nasty crappy cheap dirty fucking sex that it almost makes me cry and want to lose my mind, so maybe it's better just not to call and hope once again (as I have before but not completely successfully) that I can get her out of my heart and stop fabricating this person that she isn't and never was and never will be.

Marsha lives across the street, I rarely see her. Occasionally I hear her leave early in her Mercedes, cream-colored and a '79.

We wave as we drive by each other's modest Valley houses, and often her porch light stays on long into the day, burns until eleven or twelve, a lot longer than mine, so I know she sleeps late. It is unusual for us to talk and I prefer it that way. I don't like getting to know my neighbors; I can feel their presence, and I know if I screamed at three in the morning they would come out concerned, but there isn't any intrusion and that is exactly how I like it.

So when Marsha came by at dinnertime a few weeks back with a glass of wine in hand and quite sloshed, I was surprised, and irritated as well. But glad to have my writing interrupted, I invited her in. She looked like she had been crying, her eyes were puffy, red-rimmed and blood-shot.

I didn't really ask her why she was here, all I really knew about her was that she was an actress who I assumed did well enough to leave her porch light on long into the day.

"Jean," she said, "I hope you don't mind. I was watching you from my window, typing away, and I was drinking this wine and you looked so secure over here I just wanted to feel it for a minute . . . be close to you. I often watch you while I study my scripts and think what it must be like to be Jean—funny, smart Jean. I watch you and think that."

And with that she sat down on my Stickley rocker and began to laugh, laugh so hard she spilled wine on my Navajo rug and then looked up at me with one of the deepest saddest set of eyes I'd ever seen. I try to avoid peoples' eyes because I don't like to get that intimate with just anybody. I don't need the responsibility.

"Jean," she said again, "my mother called me and told me she cared and loved me and didn't want to be so distant anymore. I was quiet for a while and kept thinking how long I'd waited for this day and now that it was here I hated it. I was watching you while I spoke to her. 'Myrtle,' I said to her—I hate to call her Mom, 'just keep teaching those kids and loving them and sitting with your legs spread in your pantyless girdle. Teach them all your morality while they look up your dress, and don't call me twenty-five years later and expect it all to be fine. It isn't, and I'm so busy, let's just leave it as it is and we'll be friends.' Oh Jean, it wasn't good—believe me, I've waited for this for so many years, but I just didn't want it once it arrived. What do you think?"

I kept wishing I could sit at the piano and start playing so loud I could drown out her voice ringing in my head.

"Marsha, would you like a cup of coffee?"

"No, Jean, thanks, I just wanted to tell you about my conversation. I hate coffee when I'm drinking. . . . Oh Jean, by the way, maybe you could write something for me to star in. I've got great ideas."

She kissed me on the cheek and practically fell out the door, waving over her shoulder at me from across the street. She left her glass which I kicked over and broke. I wanted to curse her out, but I could see her now from my window talking on the phone, her face all balled up, so I just swept up the broken glass and went back to my writing.

he didn't try to kiss me.
he never touched my breasts
he wouldn't fuck
me
I jerked him off
he didn't come

Being young in Hollywood is redundant. Youth is all around us, blooming, on the move, intoxicated with the sweet smell of success. Fresh beauties show up in droves, and as crowded as the Hollywood scene may be, there is always room for a hot new face, a promising talent, a girl who can move and shake the agents, the producers, the directors. If only by confidence alone, a girl can make it here.

They come from everywhere. Some arrive tired and jaded off buses on Vine with scholarships to study method at Lee Strasberg, others are natives who work part time at Fred Segal's. Wherever their point of origin, there exists a new hipness and sophistication among them that was missing from my early days in town. Yes, these girls are smart but not nearly smart enough, because no one can second guess the manipulations of the Hollywood sex offenders. Let's face it, everybody wants untainted flesh, and when the promise of staring opposite Sean Penn is on the line, one might easily give up some up those scruples.

Okay, it's not quite that cliché anymore, but the bottom line is, it will always be more difficult for a woman, regardless of credentials or talent, when you're dealing with a whole business run by frustrated, short men. There is bound to be some resentment toward these beauties.

So how do you handle it, short of getting an attitude? Use some psychology. If you sense hostility coming from a casting director or fat, unattractive producer, just pretend he's your uncle and humor him. Take him into your confidence and make him feel as if it's you and him against the world. Talk about football or your favorite cocktail, guy talk, like "I've got fifty bucks on the Broncos. I think they're gonna' kick some butt. What about you?"

Don't act all girly and giggly. Be kind of tough in a sexy way, sit on the edge of the couch instead of getting comfortable, run your hands through your hair and slap him on the back. "Oh Joel, you're a scream. I love your Roseville pottery collection, it's one of the best I've ever seen. Hey, don't worry, if I'm wrong for this part we'll do something else together. I mean, I just dig you and I really want to be friends!"

Drive a motorcycle like the kind Brando rode in *The Wild One.* It's de rigeur now, so get yourself a beat-up leather jacket, some used cowboy boots, and make sure your hair is really long and definitely do not wear a helmet. Drive up and down Melrose with a cigarette hanging out of the corner of your mouth and weave confidently in and out of traffic—don't worry, you won't fall off. Show up a few minutes late and really rev your engines as you pull up for your audition at Warner Brothers—all the young execs will be scared but blown away. Talk about your record deal on Virgin; even if you don't have one, they'll believe you. Tell them you've been living in Paris, hanging out with Micky Rourke, and there's a damn good chance you'll get the job.

If you're headed for Disney lighten it just a little: Give 'em some Julia Roberts action, edgy but sweet. If in doubt, use your breasts much the way Uma Thurman does—flaunt them. Wear something sheer without a bra, they'll be so distracted you'll get the part because of the chaos you've created, but leave quickly before they figure it all out.

It's essential to develop some gay allies as well. Get in with the gay mafia, powerful producers, execs, etc. Fix them up with some of your really cute boyfriends—don't worry they won't have to do anything except act disinterested. If it doesn't work out they won't blame you, they'll just ask you to find more beautiful boys who'll reject them. Be a good friend and take their calls at six A.M. and listen while they cry the blues about how no one ever loves them, and you'll be a superstar over night!

Go to clubs, but not every week. Get everybody interested and then disappear. When you show up again they'll be so desperate they'll promise you anything and everything you want, including the Mercedes 450 SL, and baby, you deserve it.

You can date one of these guys but make sure you keep

one of his friends hanging on the line just in case. Alternate a hot actor and an older director, and maybe toss in a producer or two, and always keep an agent on hold. Get some head shots from Herb Ritts, have Sally Hershberger cut your hair, work out at Gold's Gym, and sleep late. That's my best advice for you girls, you hot, happening, groovy stars of today. Play by their rules and you'll never grow old!

(Originally appeared in *People* magazine.)

She never loved me. I swear to you nothing ever happened. I bought her gifts, sunglasses like mine, patchouli-scented lotion, incense, a tiny gold hamsa from Jerusalem to keep away the evil eye.

We went to the movies, that documentary about Klaus Barbie. I fell asleep on her lap, she lightly rubbed my head, like someone trying to get a genie out of me. I sat in her living room that smelled like the gardenias floating in big glass bowls. There were fresh flowers everywhere. I remember waiting for her with those flowers all around me.

She wore cut off jeans, men's suits, things that showed her breasts. We ate in restaurants, Caesar salads, French fries, pasta. She adored me in public more than anywhere else, where maybe someone would overhear our conversation and imagine something was really going on between us. I listened to her stories dusted off, the past deleted, shaky, unclear, like a woman without a dream looking to borrow someone else's until that, too, lost its luster and she could move on to a new one. I wanted to grab her by the shoulders and shake her until she cried. Nothing would have been more satisfying than to see her break down. I dreamed that I would be the one to break through, to hold her in my arms as she cried and confessed everything to me.

I tried to talk to her the way I did with all my friends, but my words sounded brittle, ready to break off my tongue, as if even I didn't have the courage to tell her the truth. But by then I knew she was the kind of person who couldn't hear it anyway.

By the time our friendship ended I realized I didn't even care anymore, choosing finally to simply walk away with those memories of the few times I felt my love made any difference to her at all.

I hear she's writing poetry. Odes to sex. Stolen lovers. Broken trust. Psalms for desperation. Night after night, haunting the hallways of sleeplessness, the betrayals of fame and fortune. Searching for the myth to leave behind. If I believed she was lonely I might cry. If someone could convince me she felt even a grain of remorse I might light a candle in some cathedral. If ever once she had looked me in the eyes and revealed her pain, I might have forgiven.

It was one of the last great years on this planet. It was like a remission of nature. The air had a crystalline clarity that took your breath away and the sky a blueness that you might have seen only in some technicolor dream. I remember every day I walked through it, and all the nights I would lie on a cot in my backyard afraid to fall asleep, fearing I might miss the movement of the constellations over my head, stars we would never see again.

There had been warnings for decades that time was close to running out for us here. Everyone tried as best they could, but life had to move on, and quickly. Jets roaring by, cars stranded on the roadside, great industries ticking away, time clocks of our misguided fortune. We moved swiftly, keeping the fear at bay, raising our children, making love, visiting friends in a quiet way, always forging ahead. People caved in, dreams were tossed out the window, fortunes thrown to the wind. Everyone knew that soon none of it would matter, it was only a question of time. The same time that had been coaxed along so easily before, now became time one dreaded, and wept into.

But as we sank into apathy something strange happened: the earth repaired herself. We woke up from our hideous slumbers and there she was—proud, clean, shiny, and fresh. And we took to loving her as never before. Walking gently on those tormented beaches, lolling about in waters that only yesterday were fetid and forboding. We rode bicycles endlessly along freshly sprouted forest paths, inhaling crisp broken pine scent no one had smelled other than out of a bottle in eighty years. We took time to talk and celebrate too, lovers made love with great abandon and forgiveness. When rain misted down on us we cried with it and everything got mixed together, salt, flowing streams, our laughter, and our tears.

Everyone was taken in, the young, the old, the starving. We ate bountifully—corn, oats, rye, and wheat—and with gusto and delight. Scientists marveled and began to formulate new theories, politicians felt confident again, the judges of the land enforced the law fairly and justice really was for all.

New energy surprised us. Pretty things flowered, blossoms fell. Children sang songs, everyone commented on how strong they now grew. Men slapped one another on the back and dared to laugh heartily. I watched them, beaming with pride from porch swings freshly painted, adorned with creeping vines and sweet peas.

We wondered how it happened, but no one wanted to

think about it too much for fear it would all disappear. We talked quietly, prayerfully, tenderly; we walked endlessly in fields renewed, breathing air that the universe had shaken clean.

It was the night I confessed everything. All the people I had loved. Terrible things I had done to good people— betraying, nasty, destructive, disappointing things I had said, those I had slapped in the face, turned, walked away, and never looked back on. I cried, I puked, I laid on the floor doubled up in horrible pain. She never left my side, never said a word, never wondered if I might do the same things to her. No, she simply listened, beautifully, gently, without an ounce of judgment, as if she were no better than I. I was absolved of all my sins, as she became an incredible priest behind the confessional. I could feel only her breath as she spoke to me, its purity, its soul-cleansing honesty. I looked up to the sky, fallen like a star, its light two-million years away, praying that her love had reached me in time.

In quieter times Mel was known to throw herself wringing wet onto the restless sands of the Sahara, and stare up at the sun until she was too blind to see.

"Why, Mel, you'll drive yourself half out of your mind!"

"Why ever did you drag me to this God-forsaken hellhole?" She rolled over and looked back at Jack who had taken to wrapping his face in white scarves so that only his dark bespectacled eyes shone through.

"I never dragged you anywhere darling, you just haven't seemed to gather the strength to want to leave, and, knowing me as you do, I'll sit and rot here in this miserable stench until the buzzards pluck away at my rotting flesh. Oh no, Mel, I couldn't force you anyplace, let alone make you stay!"

He laughed and coughed intermittently, a strange hoarse cough that would lead one to believe he was very ill, until he stood and exposed the breadth of his shoulders and the strength of his arms. Or perhaps one might think he could no longer navigate his way through the crazy sands but that too was incorrect. It was his fear of time he had abandoned, lovers that had disappeared, and memories of roads untraveled that left him on uncertain footing, on shaky ground.

Overwhelming nightmares brought him to his deference to Mel, the empty space of Morocco, and a general ambiguity toward the simplest task or desire. Suddenly the world seemed as if it had shrunk, and no longer could he imagine any life beyond this desert. No more bustling afternoons in Paris sipping Pernods at the Café Flore. No grand dinners with dear friends on Park Avenue. The West End in London was like some fantasy described long ago and forgotten.

Mel brought him back to her. She stroked his head as it rested on her lap, striking the image of muse and savior.

"The world is changing, darling. Somehow we've gotten lost and can't seem to find our way to it. Do you know that sometimes when I dream I see it all quite clearly. It's quite seductive, really, but then again the future always is. Perhaps we are two people bound to the present. Do you think that's the sign of a coward or just someone who knows that too much change tears the soul apart, let alone the fragile love of two fools like us? Come Jack, let us make our way back to civilization. I'm missing home ever so much and I don't believe I can ponder all of this very much longer. I think it will all be just fine because I love you so incredibly much."

With that the sun moved suddenly, forcing shadows of

the desert across the landscape shifting in the sands, taking with it their thoughts and desire. Mel and Jack were homeward bound to a life they simultaneously feared and loved. But there was laughter falling behind them as they journeyed along.

Salvador Dali tells me that man must bend to time.

That time has melted down all around me.

A black and yellow Mariposa is leading me.

And I can only dream of her dancing on a rock in the desert, her wings spread out into the wind and sun. I watch from afar, she smiles down on me, without secrets or guile, all the drawers are open for me to look into. She floats in my arms in pools of mineral water with eyes closed, lips fiery red. I lean down to kiss her tender forehead, "you are a wise old sage" I tell her with confidence. "What does this mean?" she asks with a worried look on her face. "That you see into the past, the future, but allow the present to do what it will." She is everything to me, my girlfriend, my boyfriend, a complete spirit, the yin and the yang. She smiles for me by the Eiffel Tower and the moon is full for the fourth time, hidden behind the clouds as fireworks fall down around us. Lamenting time she flies away.

When I am sad and far away again, I will gaze upon these pictures fondly. Your face will float in and out of my mind and perhaps I might fall to sleep with these visions of you sadly, sweetly, forever etched in my memory, of our times together in all the different places we may have been or have yet to go.

I've included these unfinished pieces because I always find it interesting and revealing to see what people choose to leave out.

Reject

i don't know where i was the first time it happened but
as if it were yesterday i still can recall its colors and
smells it touched me as nothing else has since in my life
and i am haunted by the slightest memory of it at all times.
when i was little i would strand by my parents bed and watch
my mother until my presence awaken her startled she would
take me in her arms and ask me gently "baby what are you
doing here in the dark?" i felt her sleepy breath against
my neck

when they found her she was laughing
like any tiny child would be crawling
among the ruins like some miniature explorer
~~people~~ more voices called out breaking the chilling
silence and she lifted her~~self~~ up craning her
small head and began to cry for the first time
~~since~~ since the shattering impact, the fire that
had lit the darkening sky was now just embers
of molten steel and twisted beams
 a flashlight caught the only motion and sign
of life ~~that remained~~

I wonder sometimes late at night if it would'nt be better to keep myself alone
what might happen if suddenly someone was there for me always mighten i just lose all
that fear and edge that keeps me running why must i punish myself but then i have allowed
some sweetness into my life more than ever now and i can see that it is good and rich
so maybe i can let myself be loved after all.

chances are you might make it to point A -
and you could catch someone's attention
but you have to prepare yourself that unless
it is fated you may go no further
and not only that you will be doing
it completely utterly alone.

these were my manicuring days, neither glamorous or exciting reminding
me constantly of where i had come and how i could be doing what i was
doing.

If you say any word enough it ceases to have any meaning.
(This has been true for love, hope and dream.)
None the less there are fragments of all of this that remains.
In memory all is forgiven and so much sadness sifted away that I can only sit in places
I have sat before and recalled the exact same thrill and anticipation of one I had conjured
up over the ocean in some glow of a cathredral I'd yet to light candles in. If we could
take out the parts gone bad, eat around the bruises I swear it might taste as it did,
fresh, clean, sweet.

But since time has definition even if we might disagree with it, we are forced to recall
it in its' entirety.

Lips kissed for the first time are kissed forever. Utterances of love barely audible
remain uchanged or questioned the smell that rises from passion hangs indelibly, A stain
on the heart. It releases, it forgives, it turns way, certainly those desires will creep
up from every crevace one treads upon until you fall madly unrelentingly back to that
time when doubts were laughed away cried or dreamed in that sacred world we created from
need and longing. I curse the time that warped the promise that made it impossible
to ride out on the broken leg of the horse of love that was shot to be put out of its
misery.

I am calm now, so I can recall these tender scenes, but when I move in closely, I am singed
by those careless flames. I reel backward to discover my footing, firm. There is that
purity that cleanses and scotes the nearly completed circles of love.

How dare it be so easy. I mourn its simplicity. Should'nt it have been less transparent?
I can taste all the richness of this time and yet like the word, I feel as if its repetition
has left it without meaning. And I ask:

How can I have it back?

january 15, 1991 tueday

scenerio hollywood on the possible eve of destruction
i am at a vouge magazine shoot with christie turlingtun
in the hollywood hills, liz the editor who i really adore
has brought up a little body eight years old who's a
rock'n roller long hair and already a bad ass attitiude
the photographer wants him to hand christie a script in
the picture "but i don't think we brought it " he says
with a sneer, christie says " I've never seen a kid like
that he already just slumps down and says ya how are ya
with a hip handshake" i looked over at sally she knew i
was'nt impressed if he was my little boy i'd wack off that
hair and force him to watbh bambi, here we are on the night
of imenent world war and in hollywood jaded eight year olds
are posing in vouge magazine, i have a little problem with
that.

November 22. 1990 Thursday

    oh America
I am over you now
   your snow caps
   and family gatherings
no matter where I wander
    where I roam
  oh America
   you will always be my home

august II, I990 saturday

there seems to be an international conspiracy against
me at health clubs today at the roman sports center
i was juststarting to do legs and on the claf machine
when this blonde chick leaning towards dyke came marxhing
her band over to inform me thant number one i was not
allowed to work out with a walkman and number two i must
ber wearing either tight fitting bicycle pants or
long pants but no looose shotts first i asked why was it
not possible to wear a walkman in case the fire peopple come
in we are in a low buliding they will give a fine, you must
be able to hear a fire alarm, oh right i see, and no
one not even men can wear loose shorts , we have some in
the dressing room you can wear, this is all in the rules
you recieved when you joined, oh heeally well no one
spoke english until it came to taking for my 300 fucking lira
for a month but no i was'nt aware of any of these rules
and certainly no one stopped me from coming in today
she laughed ironically of course exerting her nazi dyke athourity
whifh of course i was ready to take my fist and slam it into her
average forgettable cunt face i've been feeling incrredibly
violent here in rome, the heat the smatt ass attitude the
lack of energy has gotten under my skin so i'm ready
to kick anybodies ass, she heads the way to the entrance
and hands me a rule sheet oooh i see, i'm soooooo sorry for
breaking any rules! what could have possibly gotten into me?
how can i ever make it up to you, i know you're just here to
enforce these rules because by the look of your saggy flat ass
you sure the fuck have'nt been working out too much,
then she tells me i can go in and get a pair of tight fitting
shorts, ya i'M sure i'm going to wear somebodies funkny nasty
shittin shorts bitch no i think not, no but they are not someone
elses well they are now becuase i'll bring my lily white ass
back when you are not on patrol like some rabid dog, have fun
torturing some other poor schumuck you man hating wooman baiting
bitch, by the way she was the smae one enforcing the rules about
using the "special" equipment in the othe room that's all blocked
off the versa climber, the ancient sairt masters, oh no she told
me then you have to take a apecial fittness test to use this
plus pay another I50 lira, i ran up and down the spanish stairs
and had lunch at babingtons tea room in a very deserted rome.

december 29, 1989 friday

i continue to behave like some teenage boy some song by journey comes on the radio and
i'm in love again in the most simplistic way

like the old days i've been waking up in the middle of the night staring at the clock
and thinking of you oh how i long to call you and talk softly about matters of my ever
breaking heart it always seemed like when i talked to you that none of it really mattered
at all and by the time we hung up i was laughing at myself once again and falling back
into calm dreams. so now when i awake and i know i cannot ever call you again it is only
this sense of disbelief and i try to laugh again at the memories of what you said then
and what you might of said this crazy night my hands are chapped now in this the only
winter i know because i can't sit still i keep cleaning like cobwebs hanging in corners
that i've been meaning to sweep down off the ceiling for quite some time now they scared
me because they made me feel like i was gone already and this was just some house somebody
stumbled on the door ajar they slowly walked in old books and some photos scattered all
around they open a chest of drawers to once pretty slips and lingerie they finger soft
things and sit on my bed it is cold and they read a story left in my nightstand about
you softly replacing it and walking back out closing the door for another time and discovery
everything settles once again as i left it those cobwebs readjusting in their corners
and that is why i am sweeping them down today thinking of you.

october 14, 1989 saturday
there were times and i'm not sure now how recent or distant they were
that everything had this amazing sense of romance and delicacy, i could
and often did lie in bed for hours in the morning alone floating in
and out of dream and fantasy surrounded with a warmth and sense of safety
i can still recreate when i summon it.

how to break each other down
watch our love crumble
tumble slowly like a clumsy boulder rolling down into the sea
off the cliffs of distant memory
tricks we've played to break each others spirit
see the tears fall
small drops of bitter rain that splash down my gutter
no one did it better than you
my dear friend my lover
who did it first your father your mother

is it possible just this once

to have a love i 've lived for

my whole life through

just for me to really know you

in the stillness of night when i wake alone

i can call you eight thousand miles away

can't i see you again who knows where or when

November 24, 1990 Saturday

Back at home 5 a.m. where there is truly
no where to run or hide I wonder about
life the voices around my house take
on giant proportions there is loneliness
and wonderment where is everyone I love
sleeping dreaming lunching in London
sitting up in beds of their own wondering
too

By the nineties we had all lost
some and it was beginning to seem
quite surreal

He asked me in his broken English if I was beautiful.
I'm okay, yes I'm very beautiful.....meet me at the piazza
.....there is tonight a big political actors directors my
English.....?

i found her in horrible pain at the borgheses gardens
herself being me, but exhausted of thinking and going
mad with all the same shit, i felt safer in the detachment.
so there i was walking with a photographer of morrocan
descent, to the french consulate quarters so he descrived
french morrocan we talk about this shoot for max
magazine i listen here because i am alone and things
take on a differant dimension.

she was lovely really if i could step outside of her
in the twenties in paris perhaps she would have found
a home but now in modern times her confusion blinded
her as well as me, how could i comfort her and convince
her that we were all freaks most of the time, on farms
in iowa on wall street castles in germany no one fit
it and after all it was just a temporary state of affairs
for everyone passing through trying not to leave too
much destruction in ones path, maybe someone is immortal
though who knows, if someone could be and kept it a
secret they would watch all these generations dissapear
friendless and forever sad, life would go on until it
just caved in, often i thought that way about her,
for in all her pain the calls she made in late night
terror i sensed that somehow she could figure it all
out without me, it made listening all the more urgent
somehow, becuase then it was much more than the initial
experience,oit was as if she had to create the illusion
of real first time heartbreak, unbarable lonliness,
exscrutiating fear, clear and defined i sensesed
she would have to tell these stories again to someone
not unlike myself, who by choice, kept much of herself hidden away remorseful but forevwer in movement
i loved her deeply for revealing things stranely withered
and resolved, i needed that lesson badly, but knew i
would not, unlike her have another chance to trust
or forgive lifes devistation.

Right now I'm holding onto a moment that seems impossible that breaks my heart that shakes me to the very core. I am squeezing the juice out of the moment; every precious last drop. Is this a punishment that words just won't flow as they have before? Am I so afraid of what my heart might blurt out?

LET MY PEOPLE KNOW

Many people will think I'm talking about a certain girl we all
know, but I'm not, that's another story. This is about a girl
I spent some time with, a lot of time, but I never quite got a grasp
of what she was all about, you know what I mean? No, of course not,
how could you. The last time I saw her she was dressed down--well,
at least for her anyway.

I would like a blind date with one of the great guys who makes my flight reservations on America West. He always sounds so young and enthusiastic, so strong, blond and tan; I longed to meet him and go out on a really terrific date. Maybe next time I'll arrange it.

I just need a good book I keep thinking, dinner out every night: Surround yourself with friends talk about it until you exhaust yourself, put it out of your mind, numb it any way you can, slap your own face, drive it out of your mind. But of course it creeps up once again, the fucked-up fear of having nothing to do, no one to take care of, empty pockets of time that seem impossible to fill with anything satisfying, that incredible loneliness without someone to wake up next to no matter how uncertain that might be, no matter how much torture that person may inflict on you, anything to fill that void even if it means spending your life trying to find a way to resolve it. As always I had blindly jumped into another relationship, just picked up the phone and decided to make this person the right one, without looking or feeling their presence.

I jumped into freezing cold waters, convincing myself of their warmth.

I cry for the joy of having known you and for not knowing where you are today. I needed to cry and it came out that bittersweet, lonely way that tears always do, falling down all over, dramatically. Dan, you'd laugh — or maybe not; you never really did laugh at me, but dear lord we certainly laughed together. Damn it! I don't want to stop crying for a long time. It's the only time it feels at all real anymore, because you being gone will not allow my tears to fall.

I miss you to the point of no return, and I love you like I will never love anyone again.

why once again must i put myself through the process
of disconnecting from you? what in me desires the
pain of your cruelty? my deperation to be loved by you
which is next to impossible because i think you are
incapable of the act, you've wanted me to open up to
you, not keep you at an arms distance length and you know
i've tried, but i've never been with anyone who has
had as much contempt for my very core as you, every
nuance of my makeup drives you to madness, my singing,
my joy of washing clothes, the fact that i take care
of my body, that i won't drink with you every night,
as if that's a mortal sin not enjoying liquor, that's
certainly grounds for hatred, self maybe, your fury
unleashed after midnight never ceases to have it's
affect on me, and it makes my self-centered little
tirades in the daylight seem like a will-o-the-whisp
next to your demonic regurgitations, and of course i
fall for it, like some b-horror movie that suckers me
in and then manages to keep me up all night reeling
from fear and deep subconcious terror, congratulations
you are very good at what you do, but i think it's
the next morning that shocks me the most when as if
it never even happened, you willed simply cuddle up
next to me and ask if i love you, "hold me" you moan,
never a mention of the night, like dracula, the light
of day tends to turns you benign, and yes through some
permanent kind of damage you've done to my heart I still
love you and need you and wish that you would just be
alright suddenly and accept me and allow enough love
to let me do the same, i cannot fathom why you need *understand*
to make me feel insecure, how someone could be so
detached from the reality if the situation as to think *of*
if "people just work things out and stay together it
will all be fine in the end" how? we have hours and
hours of these kinds of discussions, i mean we could
have done a seminar on our relationship for as many
times we talked about it and tried to make it work.

In those days, blondes were my nemesis--they wore pink button-down
shirts and madras skirts and leapt around the football field like
wild gazelles doing graceful air splits that exposed all that dreamy,
sought-after pussy. I hated them and longed for them, their coldness
affirmed/reinforced all my self-doubts and fears. The thoughtful way
they wore their ponytails, the precise angle their arms hung
around . . . dangling on the shoulders, as if to say, I would simply
evaporate without you to cling to. . . . It was then that I knew
I could lean on no one ever, and that shattering realization entered
me like a cold steel blade. I stood frozen in my tracks until I could
regain my equilibrium. . . . I moved on into this future ever so
carefully, tiptoeing, hoping to find satisfaction without
misrepresenting my needs and desires.

On the freeway is a truck carrying two painted white trees on the way to a set. Against a smoggy September sky I watch them race away to star in a movie.